DEATH AT KING'S CHAPEL

A HIGGINS & HAWKE MYSTERY

BOOK SIX

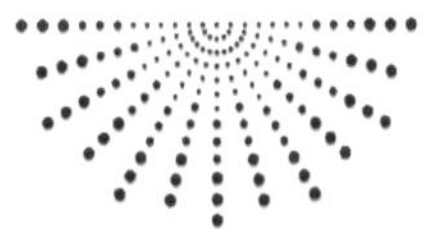

LEE STRAUSS

Death at King's Chapel

© 2024 Lee Strauss

Cover by Jordan Strauss

Cover Illustration by Tasia Strauss

Library and Archives Canada Cataloguing in Publication

Library and Archives Canada Cataloguing in Publication

Library and Archives Canada Cataloguing in Publication

Title: Death at King's Chapel / Lee Strauss.

Names: Strauss, Lee (Novelist), author.

Description: Series statement: A Higgins & Hawke mystery ; book 6

Identifiers: Canadiana (print) 20240334469 | Canadiana (ebook) 20240334477 | ISBN 9781774094976 (hardcover) | ISBN 9781774095003 (softcover) | ISBN 9781774094969 (EPUB) | ISBN 9781774094983 (Kindle) | ISBN: 978-1-77409-510-2 (bookvault) | ISBN: 978-1-77409-511-9 (d2d) | ISBN: 978-1-77409-512-6 (ingram spark)

Subjects: LCGFT: Historical fiction. | LCGFT: Novels.

Classification: LCC PS8637.T739 D42 2024 | DDC C813/.6—dc23

THE HIGGINS & HAWKE MYSTERIES

IN ORDER

Death at the Tavern

Death on the Tower

Death on Hanover

Death by Dancing

Death on Tremont Row

Death at King's Chapel

A call to visit a cemetery wasn't something out of the ordinary. As Boston's chief medical examiner, Dr. Haley Higgins' job was advocating for the dead and providing answers for the living. Haley lived and breathed forensic science, and the 1930s looked promising for new breakthroughs in the field, which could only help her do her best at her job.

With many of the first settlers making their home in Boston, the city had some of the oldest burying grounds in the country, and King's Chapel's burying ground was the oldest of those.

Parking her '29 DeSoto on Tremont, Haley grabbed her medical bag and walked across the grounds to the church entrance, where she'd agreed to meet Detective Brock. The cemetery's grand prestige didn't match its actual size. The old plot held rows of tilted, weather-worn headstones like crooked teeth. The lawns surrounding them were well kept, and the trees and bushes were trimmed and pruned. The shade created there kept the grass soft and damp, and it squished under Haley's weight.

The crypt lay underneath the chapel, and Haley found the now familiar form of Nolan Brock waiting inside, his shoulders slouching as if to compensate for his above-average height—a temptation Haley knew well, being overly tall herself. His hat, dented at the front, sat slightly askew on a round head. Although some considered him physically and socially awkward, Haley found him endearing. And, to her dismay, she now considered his nicely symmetrical face rather attractive. Even more concerning was how her cheeks grew warm when he acknowledged her with a tip of his hat and how she impulsively responded by pushing runaway curls behind her ears.

"Dr. Higgins," Detective Brock said.

"Detective." Their initial conversation was brief, as they'd just gotten off the telephone with each other. During the call, Detective Brock had made Haley aware of a grim discovery.

Haley greeted his accompanying officers before taking in the sanctuary of King's Chapel.

Considering the Romanesque multi-column exterior, the interior was plain, with white-washed walls and pillars. A couple of simple chandeliers hung from ceilings, with wooden boxed seating instead of pews below them.

The minister's secretary, a serious, thin-faced man, talked as he led the group down the stone steps. "We've got electrical lighting upstairs, but we still rely on oil lamps down here."

The door to the crypt was opened, the mouth lit by the oil lamps.

Detective Brock picked up one of the lamps. "Normally, I'd say ladies first, but perhaps it would be best if I lead the way down."

Haley didn't protest, carefully following the detective, once again thankful that her height kept her from purchasing fashionable high-heeled shoes —a style that had come into vogue for women over the previous few years.

"Have you been down already?" Haley asked.

Detective Brock looked even taller in the crypt. His hat brushed against a ceiling beam that pushed the fedora off his head. He bent with bony knees to retrieve it. "Yes, but I didn't touch anything and gave firm directives that no one else touch anything either."

"In no way did I suspect you to be guilty of tampering with the scene of a possible crime, Detective," Haley quickly replied.

"I didn't mean to imply that you did. It's worth stating so for the record."

The tomb opened at the bottom of the steps. The remains of those buried were hidden behind a brick wall, and Haley could only presume the decision to do so in the last century had been for preservation. Stone-carved nameplates were mounted on the brick surface, identifying the individuals on the other side, such as William Emerson, Elizabeth Pain, and John Winthrop. However, many names had worn away with time.

Haley swallowed hard as a drop of perspiration worked its way down the back of her neck and spine. Detective Brock held the lamp's bright light in front of her face, and she blinked. "Are you all right, Dr. Higgins?"

Haley placed a palm to her heart, willing the beat to slow. "Yes. Fine. I'm a little claustrophobic."

"I see. Well, let's hurry with it then, shall we?"

Detective Brock held the lamp over the remains that had brought Haley to the tomb in the first place.

She focused on what was left of the body—the bones wrapped in linen. She pushed back the blackness of the walls and imposed an imagined field around them instead, lying to herself that the dank air she breathed in came from damp fields after a recent rainfall.

"How often is the crypt inspected?" Haley asked.

"According to the secretary, the groundskeeper, who doubles as a custodian, comes in at least once a month. Just for a sweep and dusting. There hasn't been a new placement here since 1895."

Haley studied the victim. "It looks as if it was placed here with purpose, not simply tossed down the steps."

"This vault may be of some significance." The detective moved the oil lamp along the bricked-in wall and ran a finger along a name plate at eye level. "This one says General something or other. They've been down here for ages, and the etching is hard to make out." He turned to face Haley. "Can you tell me anything from this first cursory observation?"

"Hold the lamp closer, please." Haley tugged on her skirt and squatted by the corpse. She produced a pencil from her medical bag, shifted the ragged-looking sheath with the tip, and uncovered the bones. "Male, I'd say. Probably stabbing."

"You can tell that from just looking?"

"The male cranium is larger with pronounced brow and jaw. The subcostal angle of the ribs—the angle formed where the lower ribs meet the sternum —is sharper in males and the sternum is typically longer and thicker, both demonstrated here. Two ribs have distinct nicks, possibly from a knife or some sort of blade. I'll be able to tell you more once the bones have been brought to my morgue."

Standing, she caught her breath. The illusion of the open field had evaporated, and the sense of walls closing in pressed against her chest. She didn't even register that Detective Brock had taken her hand and was leading her up the stairs to the open space of the sanctuary.

Haley headed straight outside and, once there, took several breaths. She blinked in the view of the burying ground, the rows of jagged headstones—as beautiful to her as any pastoral view.

"Doctor?"

Haley turned to Detective Brock's voice; his dark brow raised in concern.

Embarrassed by apparent weakness, Haley pushed her shoulders back and forced a smile. "I'm fine. I promise. Do you need me for anything else?"

"I think I can carry on without your presence, Dr.

Higgins. You can expect delivery of the remains in short order."

After a curt nod, Haley turned on her heel and headed across the burying ground, zigzagging around the ancient headstones until she reached her car. She still felt out of sorts as she maneuvered through traffic—a mix of rumbling motorcars and the slower horse-and-buggy contraptions—until she was parked again, this time at Massachusetts General Hospital at the corner of Allen and Charles.

Dr. Thomas Martin, who, in Haley's opinion, looked too youthful for his position, was seated at his desk inside the entrance of the morgue. A slim man in his late twenties, he was clean-shaven with hair trimmed short at the neck and temples and longer on top, parted sharply from one side.

"You appear a bit flustered, Dr. Higgins," he said. "Is everything all right?"

Haley huffed. She should've taken a minute to examine her appearance in the rearview mirror. Removing her hat, she used her fingers to tidy her hair, fighting with the ponytail she typically wore.

"There's a body coming," she said without answering her assistant's question.

Dr. Martin jumped to his feet. "I'll prepare for the autopsy. Did you want me to start the Y incision?"

"That won't be necessary for this, Dr. Martin. I hope you paid attention in your classes on osteology."

Dr. Martin gazed back at Haley with interest. "Is there something special about the bones in this case?"

"You could say that." Haley relayed the news about the body in the crypt. "The interesting thing is that the body was recently moved there. Whoever did it must've known the groundskeeper would eventually discover it."

"If we're talking bones, then the body had to have been kept somewhere all this time."

"Yes, I'd say at least a year. Detective Brock has an interesting case on his hands."

Haley went to her office, which had a glass wall facing the morgue. It gave her a good view of the space, brighter than one would think a basement area could be due to the white-painted walls and ceiling and the installation of electric lights. A ceramic surgical table sat in the middle of the room. Dr. Martin wiped it down with disinfectant to prepare for the new arrival. He angled the large cone-shaped lamp overhead. Shelves had all the equipment needed for the work done in a morgue, such as Bunsen burners, test tubes, measuring utensils, and drawers with scalpels, tongs, and spatulas.

Though Haley appreciated the view of her morgue as she sat at her desk doing paperwork, she wouldn't have minded a little privacy. She rarely wore makeup, but it wasn't like she didn't engage in a bit of vanity and would like to give her mop a good brushing. Her hair had been the bane of her existence since childhood. The genetics for curly hair were strong in her family. Her parents both had dark curls, a trait passed on to her and her three older brothers. They, at least, kept their locks short and weren't bothered by the odd curl. On the other hand, Haley found caring for her hair to be more work than caring for a child.

She shook her head. That thought was over-dramatic.

Now that she had an actual child living under her roof, she couldn't continue to make that unfair comparison. Her roommate, Samantha Rosenbaum, was a single mother raising a young daughter. She was the one who had to work hard, juggling parenting and work as a reporter at *The Boston Daily Record*. Putting up with those jokers at the paper wasn't even the half of it. Though it wasn't unheard of to find women working in journalism in these modern times, they were few. A lot of vitriol was shot Sam's way for *taking a man's job*.

Haley was proud of her friend, who had repeatedly dealt with public pressure and proved herself worthy. Investigative journalism wasn't an easy line of work.

Thinking about Samantha . . . Haley wondered if she should call her. Certainly, there was a story here. It wasn't every day a nearly decomposed body was randomly found in a crypt.

However, Detective Brock might frown on that. As chief medical examiner, Haley worked closely with the police. It was her duty to consider things from their perspective first, and she knew the police loathed involving the press.

However, the press would be involved; it was inevitable. And why shouldn't Samantha get the break?

Haley was saved from making an immediate decision on her dilemma by the ringing of the bell. The body had arrived.

Samantha had become so used to the newsroom, known as the bullpen, of *The Boston Daily Record* that she didn't even register the off-putting smells of cigarette smoke, body odor, and dankness that came with old brick buildings. The din of typewriter clatter and the distant ringing of rotary telephones didn't break her concentration anymore, especially when on a deadline. Despite having turned in the story of the week about a murder at a local theater, she was still expected to keep up with the fluff pieces for the ladies' pages. Penny-pinching was a popular topic, so Samantha couldn't go wrong with recipes that stretched to feed many mouths without breaking the bank. The classic beans cooked in molasses was always a favorite, but women everywhere already knew how to make that by heart. Samantha had to think of a way to make it stand out. She'd heard Mrs. Berrymaple, the neighbor who cooked for them and helped to look after Sam's daughter Talia, mention putting sliced wieners into the pot. That was a spin a woman on a tight budget would want.

"Hey, Hawke!"

Johnny Milwaukee's voice pulled Samantha's mind back into the room. Slowly, she turned in her chair to face him. "Johnny, can't you see I'm busy? *Someone* has to do some work around here."

Johnny grinned as he tossed a crumpled-up piece of paper into the nearest trash can, evidence that maybe she *was* the only one hard at work.

"Freddy here wants to bet me fifty cents that his horse, Hotshot, will win the Kentucky Derby. What do you think?"

Samantha shrugged. "I think it's a bunch of nonsense. Gambling—money down the drain."

"It is," Johnny admitted. He leaned back in his chair and tented his fingers. "Pure belly wash."

"What's a dame gonna know about horseracing?" Fred Hall muttered.

"Well, most dames might know nothin', but Sam ain't no ordinary dame."

Samantha's breath caught in her throat, and she turned back to her typewriter. She never knew how to take Johnny's jesting. He liked her, sure, even stood up for her when the fellas in the room let their bigotry show. But she'd done something foolish. She'd let herself fall in love with him.

She had no shot; Sam knew this. Not only was she a widow, but she was a widow with a child. No fella wanted a ready-made family. And besides, Johnny had a gal. Miss Betty Melrose.

"Leave her alone, Milwaukee."

Samantha's gaze shot across the pen to the speaker that came to her defense. Behind the desk sat a relative newcomer, Doug Wallenburg, known casually as Wally. He pushed up on his wire-framed glasses and grinned.

Samantha glanced away. She hadn't needed to be saved by the man, and she certainly wasn't going to encourage him. Taking a long breath, she forced herself to concentrate. Beans, beans. Beantown, one of Boston's nicknames, came from the story about all the beans and molasses the pilgrims ate when they'd settled there. Should she add that tidbit to her piece? Why not?

Just as her fingers started racing along the keys of her black Remington typewriter, the telephone on her desk rang. Yes, *on her desk*. She'd been the only reporter without her phone for many months, but after turning in a couple of good stories, her editor, Archie August, decided she'd earned one.

"Hello, Samantha Hawke speaking."

The headmaster of Talia's school was on the other end. Samantha's heart skipped. "Is Talia all right?"

"Yes, Mrs. Rosenbaum. She fell in the schoolyard and hurt her knee. I think it's her pride that's been bruised. She's asking to go home, and since, well, there is a bit of blood present, I thought I should call you."

Samantha pinched her eyes together. It was the middle of the afternoon, and Mr. August expected a couple more hours of work from her. Talia came first; of course she did, but Mr. August would dock Samantha's pay if she left early. Even though she had more money now, thanks to her late husband's nefarious activities, she still lived month to month.

"Are you sure she's not hurt badly?" Samantha asked. "Because if she is, I'll be down there immediately."

"She's upset, but it's nothing that won't heal."

"I'll call my neighbor, Mrs. Berrymaple. She'll come for Talia."

"Yes, we know Mrs. Berrymaple. She's brought Talia to school before occasionally, of course. Would you like me to call her for you? You sound busy."

Samantha's focus broadened from the voice on the phone to the noise in the room behind her, which made her sound very busy. "If you don't mind, that would save me a lot of trouble."

"Not at all, Mrs. Rosenbaum. Thank you for your time."

"Thank you."

Samantha let the receiver fall onto the cradle, her chest tight with guilt. She pictured little blond-haired Talia, with her skinny arms and legs, one knobby knee bleeding and bandaged, and tears in her round blue eyes. Dang it all. Sometimes, life wasn't fair.

"Hey, doll." Johnny sauntered over, fists tucked into his pockets, and rested against Samantha's desk when he reached it. "Is everything okay?"

"Sure," Samantha said, her hand moving her long blond bob, patting the lower curls. "Just swell."

The way Johnny stared at her—his hair oiled with a sharp side part, his clean-shaven face and crooked grin—made her knees weaken. "Don't you got something to do?" she said abruptly.

Her brashness never seemed to faze Johnny. He

laughed. "Always, doll." Then he sauntered back to his desk, Fred Hall giving him a dirty look for conversing with the enemy. Samantha wondered about the surly sportswriter. Some gal had to have stomped on his cold heart with a pointed stiletto heel somewhere down the line. Definitely not a fan of the female species. Samantha couldn't help but feel sorry for the man's wife.

Max Owen, a photographer working for the paper, stepped into the pen. The young man was so shy it had taken him months before he spoke to Samantha. Maybe his shyness was what drove him to pick up a camera—his shield to capture society without having to engage in it. He dropped a folder on Johnny's desk.

"These from the last city council meeting?" Johnny asked.

Max nodded.

Johnny slapped Max on the back, his exuberance causing Max to nearly lose his footing.

"Really, Johnny," Samantha spat. "You can be such a brute."

"Take it easy, doll. Mr. Owen knows I got his back. Thanks again for snapping these."

Max nodded and turned on his heel, heading back the way he had come, most probably from the darkroom on the floor below, next to the composing and the printing press crew.

"Slow news day," Johnny said. "Harvard's presidency might be opening up. A couple of professors are vying for the job." He waved a palm. "Any takers?"

Suddenly, the phones began to ring, one after the other. This usually meant one thing: a story was breaking. Each reporter had their own contacts in the city, including some cops and telephone operators.

The reporters in the room each picked up their own ringing phone. Johnny picked up his.

Samantha stared forlornly at her own phone, quiet and still. Since parting ways with Officer Tom Bell, she no longer had a contact on the force. She'd need to rectify that soon. For a short while, she'd had an alliance with Detective Brock, and they agreed to "scratch each other's back," but he wasn't going to contact her about a lead.

But it wasn't like she didn't have anyone. She had Haley. Was it possible that a story was breaking that Haley didn't know about? Maybe if it concerned politics or some other social scandal. That must be it. Haley could only give her leads on murders.

Samantha stared at Johnny as he grabbed his hat and coat. "What is it?" she asked.

"Sorry, doll. Gotta keep it under my hat for now."

Samantha waved a hand at all the other men racing out behind him. "I think it's out of your hat, Johnny."

Helpless, Samantha watched the room empty out until it was only vile Fred Hall and her alone in the pen.

"Do you know what it's all about, Freddy?"

Fred shrugged. "Nope."

Mr. August stepped into the pen, his eyes narrowing at the empty seats. "They heard about the mayor, I guess."

"What about the mayor?" Samantha asked.

"Called a press conference. Word is Councilman Daniel Irwin is running against him in the next election."

Samantha slumped in her seat. Whatever the mayor had to say, the story would print without her byline. Just as well. She had the bean piece to finish.

It only took her fifteen minutes to type it up, then walk to Mr. August's office to drop it on his desk. He looked up at her over his spectacles, smoke from his cigar spiraling to the ceiling.

"It's the piece for the ladies' page, sir," she said.

He nodded with a grunt, and she returned to her desk.

Freddy seemed busy with something. The Red Sox, probably. Folks who liked sports couldn't get enough of Babe Ruth.

Samantha tapped her painted-pink fingernails on the top of her desk. She should've gone to pick up Talia. They could be having a good jaw over cookies and milk right now. Maybe she should call Mrs. Berrymaple to ensure everything was all right.

Mr. August frowned on personal use of the company telephones. Samantha hesitated, picked up the receiver, and asked the operator to connect her to the Grove apartment telephone number. It rang twice before Mrs. Berrymaple's voice came on the line.

"Higgins and Rosenbaum residence," she sang.

Samantha turned her back to the pen and lowered her voice. "Mrs. Berrymaple, it's me. Did the school call you about picking up Talia?"

"They did. Caught me just as I was about to leave for the Boston Historical Society. Talia and Mr. Midnight are enjoying a little snack as we speak."

"I'm sorry you missed out on—what was it again?"

"Boston Historical Society. They're working to

preserve Boston's unique historical sites, like Paul Revere's home and the Old North Church. It's surprising what people are willing to tear down for the sake of progress."

"I've heard about the society," Sam said.

"It's been around for a while but doesn't have a lot of funding or influence. They're hoping to change this. Mrs. Jones on the second floor invited me to join. I agreed to go for the tea and cake she promised would be there, but I found I quite liked the ladies. It's something to do."

"Well, thanks again," Samantha said. She'd have to keep Mrs. Berrymaple's social calendar in mind going forward. "See ya later."

The receiver had only been sitting on the cradle of the telephone for a moment before it rang. It was still warm when Samantha picked it up.

"Sam Hawke here."

"Samantha, it's Haley."

Samantha straightened in her chair. Haley never called just to chat. "Hi, Haley. Do you have something for me?"

"I do. Can you come to the morgue?"

"On my way!" Samantha placed her hat carefully on her head and then grabbed her handbag.

"Where you goin' now?" Fred said with a scowl.

"The mayor will be done by now. 'Fraid you missed that story."

"There's always another story, Mr. Hall," Samantha said. For a moment, she felt bad about leaving the man alone in the pen, but the feeling quickly dissipated. With a smirk, she turned on her heel, and headed out.

CHAPTER THREE

"This is what I call a bag of bones," Dr. Martin said as he sorted the bones found in the crypt across the surface of the surgical table.

Haley opened her mouth, preparing to reprimand him for showing a lack of respect for the dead, but then clamped her lips shut. Her assistant was a doctor in his own right and a peer of sorts, even if she had seniority over him in this present work situation. However, his youth did betray him regularly, especially when he opened *his* mouth.

"Can't recall another case like this," he continued, "at least not on my watch."

"It's preferable to be found quickly upon dying, I would think," Haley said, setting the skull at the top of the table, then searching for the vertebrae and setting them up in proper order.

Dr. Martin placed the clavicles along the horizontal lines of the imaginary shoulders. "Appears to be male," he said.

"I concur," Haley said.

Before long, they had the bones set out on the table in their proper positions, right down to all the many bones of the hands and feet. The narrow pelvic area and the heart-shaped inlet pointed to a male victim, as did the sloping forehead of the skull, along with the robust brow ridge and stronger chin.

Dr. Martin grunted.

"What is it?" Haley said as she placed the last bone of the right little toe.

"There appears to be a phalange missing?"

Haley looked up. "Oh, which one?"

"The tip of the little finger of the right hand."

"Check the bag," Haley instructed, nodding to the small black body bag in which the bones had been transported. "And the linen the bones were wrapped in."

Dr. Martin did as he was told, then shook his head. "Not here."

"I hope nothing was left in the crypt."

"Maybe the fella lost it somehow. Dr. Martin

said. "Many folks are getting their fingers pinched with these heavy car doors."

"Let's not speculate, Dr. Martin. You can begin documenting."

Dr. Martin collected a notebook and pencil and began jotting down details of their findings.

"The spine appears to be deformed," Haley said. "Look at how it curves here."

"Spinal tuberculosis?"

"Looks like it."

A knock at the door was followed by Detective Brock's entrance. Holding his dented fedora in one hand, he grinned as he said, "May I come in?"

"Of course," Haley said. "We've just laid out the bones. Dr. Martin and I are about to record our findings, but I can give you a cursory overview."

"That would be tremendous. This one is such a puzzle. Uncle Emmet wishes he could take the lead, but he's bound to desk work for now."

Haley grimaced. Detective Emmet Cluney wasn't what you'd call easygoing, and though he didn't mind sitting, Haley could guess he didn't like being told that was what he had to do.

"It takes a while after an appendectomy to get back on your feet," Haley said. "What will happen to you when he does? Will you be moved off homicide?"

Detective Brock, a recent import from Delaware, had joined the Boston Police Department and had been moved into homicide when Detective Cluney had ended up in the hospital.

"Not sure," he said. "Violent crime is up, so they may have me stay. Depends on if I do a good job with a case, maybe."

Haley nodded. She'd had her doubts when she'd first met Nolan Brock, put off by his brashness and what appeared to be rudeness, but had come to understand that he never meant offense. It was a quirk of his personality, which seemed to work well with his detection style.

"So, what do you know?" he asked.

"Male in his forties." Haley had determined this by the level of joint corrosion, and wear of the tooth enamel. She continued, "He was five foot seven at the time of death."

Detective Brock narrowed his gaze. "Why do you say at the time of death?"

"He had a disease of the spine, something like spinal tuberculosis. The spine curved over time, reducing his overall height. With a normal spine, he'd be closer to five-nine.

"Interesting."

"A standard calculation is the length of the humerus—"

"The arm bone?"

"Yes, the long bone from shoulder to elbow, multiplied by five."

"Five times the length of an arm bone gives you a man's height?"

"Or woman's."

Detective Brock held out his long arm and stared at it with interest.

Haley held in a grin. "Of course, since we have the entire skeleton, we simply measured from head to heel with a measuring tape."

"Right. So, a male in his forties, about five foot seven." He placed a long finger on his chin. "At the crypt, you mentioned you thought the victim was stabbed. Do you still believe that?"

Haley pointed to the visible nicks in the two right-side back ribs. "Yes. The damage is clearer in this light. He was stabbed in the back, through the heart."

"No chance of survival there," Detective Brock said grimly. "And how long has he been dead?"

"Time of death is more difficult to determine with any precision," Haley said. "Older bones are dry and often discolored, depending on where they have been stored. You can see the glossiness that remains on these, which tells me the death probably occurred a year ago or so. At least a year for decomposition to be this far advanced."

Detective Brock rubbed the back of his neck. "Won't be long before word gets out to the press."

Samantha was already aware, but Haley kept this information to herself.

"Are you going to release anything official?" she asked.

"Not yet. Don't know anything." He paused, then added, "So the death happened probably sometime last spring? Say April or May 1931?"

"Give or take." Haley folded her arms. "Are you aware of any missing persons from that time?"

Detective Brock worked his lips and shook his head. "I wasn't around but got officers checking into that for me now."

"Will you let me know if you come across anything?"

The detective stilled. "I suppose I will. 'Course, I'm more apt to over dinner, if you're willing."

Haley had made the mistake in the past of thinking offers from Detective Brock to share a meal were invitations to go on a date when, in reality, the detective had a healthy appetite and liked to kill two birds with one stone, so to speak.

"I'm open," Haley said, without committing.

Detective Brock slammed his fedora on his head, and Haley wondered how much longer the hat could take such abuse. "I'll leave the both of you to it, then. Good day, Doctor." Then to Dr. Martin, "Doctor."

The detective marched out of the morgue without another look, not even bothering to ensure the door had closed behind him, which it hadn't.

Dr. Martin crossed the room to close it. "Strange fella, isn't he? But that's the police for ya. A strange lot." He hadn't taken two steps when the door opened again.

CHAPTER FOUR

"Haley!" Samantha said, blowing into the room like the wind. Her cheeks were rosy as if she had run down the steps to the hospital basement, which she probably had. She had a natural exuberance and an innate drive, which was part of why she was so good at her job.

"Samantha, thanks for coming."

"Of course." Her blue eyes stared at Haley, round and bright. "I know you wouldn't have asked me to come unless you had a reason." She took a quick breath. "You do have a reason, don't you?"

"I do, actually." Haley waved toward the ceramic surgical table and smiled at Sam's quizzical response. From where they stood, the table looked empty, or at least void of a corpse.

"Hello, Miss Hawke," Dr. Martin said shyly.

Samantha's spring dress was striking, a slimming number in pale green with a flowing skirt that landed mid-shin, a thin contrasting belt, and a matching long-sleeved, short-waisted jacket. Her black broad-brimmed hat made her blond hair stand out like a halo, and her black T-strap shoes clicked happily as she strolled along the tile floor. Thomas had that puppy-dog look many men got when appreciating the beauty of the opposite sex. Haley frowned. Her assistant and his lady friend had only recently parted ways. It wouldn't hurt him to take a little breather before a new pursuit, would it?

"Hello, Doctor," Samantha said. "So, what's up?" She stepped closer, and her mouth opened. "Oh. What's this?"

Dr. Martin sauntered over, his hands casually inside the pockets of his lab coat. "Skeletal remains," he said. "A murder."

"Dr. Martin," Haley said, exasperated.

Her assistant had the decency to look sheepish. "I apologize for overstepping." He smiled in Samantha's direction. "It's not my place to present findings."

"Why don't you take our samples to the laboratory, Dr. Martin?" Haley said, looking at her assistant sharply.

"Right, yes." He turned to the table that held the tray of vials. "Right away."

When he was gone, Haley turned to Samantha. "Sorry about that."

"It's okay. I deal with much worse than that every day."

"But you should be safe here," Haley snorted. "I'll have a talk with Dr. Martin about professional behavior."

Samantha waved her fingers, her long painted nails creating a pink blur in the air. "No need on my account. Besides, he's kinda cute."

Haley frowned. If they were sitting around her kitchen table or in the living room of her apartment, Haley might probe more about the comment. Had Samantha's feelings for Johnny Milwaukee faded?

"These bones were discovered in the crypt of King's Chapel," she said.

"Good golly, Haley!" Samantha's eyes brightened. "What a scoop!"

"Hold your horses, Sam. Nothing I'm sharing with you here has been released to the press."

"Then why am I here?"

"Because it will be eventually, and I wanted to run some things by you."

Samantha pursed bright red lips. "All right. Shoot."

"Did your paper ever run a story about a missing person?"

"Probably," Samantha said. "It happens from time to time."

"This would be late '30 to spring of '31."

"Male, female?"

"Male, in his forties."

"Doesn't ring a bell, but I was kinda busy with my life falling apart, so I might not have registered it. I can take a look." She nodded at the table. "I'm assuming you found him and are looking for a name."

"And a motive for murder."

"Ah, so Dr. Martin was right. How'd the poor fella die?"

"Stabbed in the back through the heart. From what we can tell, he also lost the tip of a baby finger along the way."

"I appreciate the lead," Samantha said tentatively. "Because, you know, I must write this up, especially if I find the victim's name."

"Naturally," Haley said. "I just don't want to jump the gun, to step on any toes."

Samantha grinned. "Would these toes happen to belong to a handsome young detective?"

Haley scowled. "His, Cluney's, the entire precinct's toes. We have to stay on their good side if we want in on their cases."

"Just pullin' your leg, Haley. What does Detective Brock have to say?"

"Not much. I told him what I know about the bones so far."

"So, you scratched his back, and he left without scratching yours?"

"Is there a reason you're being vulgar, Sam?"

"No, it's just that I thought he and I had an agreement to help each other, but I think that might've been a onetime thing. Anyway, I'm going home. Should I tell Mrs. Berrymaple you'll be back for supper?"

Haley nodded. "I'll head there once Dr. Martin returns from the lab. Just a few things to finish up."

Samantha wiggled her fingers. "See ya later, then."

CHAPTER FIVE

Haley loved living in the North End. The waterfront was nearby, no matter what part of the district you were in. The Charles River and the Charles River Esplanade, a gorgeous three-mile-long park, was only five blocks west of her Grove Street apartment. Another convenience was the proximity of the hospital to the north and the police precinct she passed by along the way. The weather in New England had been unseasonably warm lately, prompting Haley to enjoy a walk to work rather than deal with the morning traffic rush. On impulse, she decided to drop in at the precinct. Now that Detective Cluney was back at work, she might as well talk to him.

The attending officer at the front desk smiled. "Good morning, Dr. Higgins."

"Good morning, Officer Bell."

Officer Thomas Bell was a fine policeman and a onetime love interest of Samantha's, though a romance had never actually got off the ground. "Is Detective Cluney in?"

"Indeed, Doctor. Though . . ."

Haley stepped closer to the officer as he lowered his voice. "Just warning you—he's a bit of a bear."

Haley laughed. "I expected nothing less."

The precinct was as nondescript as they came, with square rooms, plain walls, and scuffed-up floors.

Haley tapped on the door to Detective Cluney's office and stepped inside after hearing the gruffly spoken "Come in."

"Hello, Detective." The room was small but larger than most in the building, with a large desk covered in papers, an overfull ashtray, and a half-full coffee mug. A rickety fan made a weak attempt of blowing air about the room. "Good to see you up and about."

Detective Cluney wore a short-sleeved shirt with a tie loosened at the collar. A set of suspenders made grooves in the fleshiness of his round shoulders. He stared at her and harrumphed. "Dang incision won't heal properly. I'm sittin' in this chair for show. And this heat, gol darn it."

Haley took the empty chair in front of her and picked up a folded newspaper sitting on the desk to use as a fan. The humidity was almost unbearable. She glanced at the open window and let out a breath of frustration at how little it helped to cool the room off.

"Why don't you go on a real holiday?" Haley said when the detective shifted uncomfortably.

"Everyone thinks I've already been gone two weeks."

That was what he got for lying about being in the hospital with appendicitis, Haley thought, but the man's pride wasn't her business.

"How's the family?" Haley asked, glancing at the single photograph of the detective's kids in the room.

"They're fine, Dr. Higgins. Please don't tell me you're here to shoot the breeze. Believe it or not, I got work to do."

"I believe it. I'm wondering about those bones found in the crypt."

Detective Cluney raised a bushy brow. "Is there a

reason you're not jawin' with my nephew right now instead of wastin' my time?"

"I thought he was here as a temporary replacement for you?"

"Do I look like I can do field work? Nah, Nolan's on that case." He shifted uncomfortably. "What, you don't like him?"

Haley was taken aback. "I never suggested such a thing."

"Then go talk to him. He got here just a few minutes before you did. I'm sure he'd love to be bothered."

Haley pushed to her feet. She was used to Detective Cluney's brash manner and had come to find it endearing. "I will. Thank you. I hope the rest of your day remains as pleasant." She thought she saw a hint of a smile before the detective returned to the paperwork in front of him.

JUST AS DETECTIVE CLUNEY had said, Nolan Brock was in his office. His greeting was more agreeable than his uncle's.

"Dr. Higgins! Come in!"

"Hello, Detective. I hope you don't mind my

dropping in like this. The hazard of the precinct being on my path to the morgue."

"Not at all." Detective Brock motioned to the empty chair for Haley to claim before he took his own. He loosened his tie before using his handkerchief to mop his brow. "If it's this hot in May, I don't know how we'll stand the summer."

"The weather's unusual. I've heard a report that it will cool off soon."

Detective Brock chuckled. "What a job, huh? Look out the window and tell people the weather. If only our jobs were so easy." He leaned in. "Do you have more to tell me about the bones?"

"I'm afraid not. I was hoping you found something that pointed to the victim's identity. I do hate calling them John or Jane Doe."

The detective shook his head. "Nothing yet. Turns out people go missing all the time. There's a big file to go through. I gotta man looking for missing forty-year-old males dating back ten or so years."

"I'm sure it's a haystack," Haley said, fanning herself with the newspaper she hadn't left behind in Detective Cluney's office. "What do you know about the crypt itself? Who has regular access to it? Or any access at all."

Detective Brock leaned back in his chair. "Are you sure you're in the right profession, Dr. Higgins? Maybe you should join the force. They're taking a few women on now."

Haley pursed her lips. "I'm satisfied with my choice of profession, Detective. Samantha told me that you like to scratch backs. I thought we had that understanding."

With a sigh, Detective Brock relaxed his shoulders, then took off his suit jacket. "I hope you don't mind, but I'm fryin' in this thing."

"Not at all."

"All right, Dr. Higgins. I'll agree to a back-scratching arrangement with you. As far as I can ascertain, there is one groundskeeper, Manfred Cole, who manages the burying grounds and oversees the crypt. We've learned from Mr. Cole that members of the Boston Historical Society have requested access for documentation purposes."

"My housekeeper is a new member of that society," Haley said. "I can ask her about it. Who were the members that viewed it?"

Detective Brock flipped through his notepad. "A Mr. William Turner and a Mrs. Berrymaple. Isn't she your housekeeper?"

"She is," Haley returned. Giving a positive spin,

she continued, "A serendipitous turn of events as she'll be able to give me a firsthand accounting of what she saw." Feeling the need to change the subject, she added, "And what about the press? Isn't it time to bring them in before it gets leaked?"

"I suppose it is news," Detective Brock said. "Maybe someone will provide information to help discover who this poor fella is." Rubbing his chin, he added, "I suppose you want to give the story to Miss Hawke?"

"It seems fair," Haley said. Sam was waiting for her permission to run with the story, and Haley was eager to give it.

"Right, the back-scratching thing," Detective Brock said. "Should I call her, or do you wanna do it?"

"It might be best if I do, in case she's not the one to answer her telephone. Her coworkers would be very suspicious if one of them took a message from the police. They're used to me calling."

"Very well, Dr. Higgins. But tell her to keep the tidbit about the little finger out of print. We don't want to reveal all of our cards just yet."

Haley stood, leaving the worn newspaper on the seat of her chair. "Thank you, Detective."

Detective Brock also stood and smiled in that

crooked manner that Haley was starting to find endearing.

"Doctor," he started, "I'm going to find Mr. Turner from the Boston Historical Society and have a chat. Would you like to accompany me?"

Haley held back the smile that threatened. "I'd be happy to."

CHAPTER SIX

The Boston Historical Society kept a small office near Faneuil Hall. It was a gamble whether they'd find anyone on the premises, and if they did, would Mr. Turner be there?

Sometimes, the die does fall in your favor—Mr. Turner was the clerk on duty when Haley and Detective Brock arrived.

The detective made quick introductions, holding his dented hat loosely in one hand. "Mr. Turner, could you explain why you and a Mrs. Berrymaple requested access to the crypt at King's Chapel Burying Ground?"

Mr. Turner, a diminutive man with round cheeks and deep smile lines, said, "Just routine, sir. The

Boston Historical Society aims to record all properties of a certain age. We detail current condition and record recommendations for preservation purposes."

"When was that?"

Mr. Turner's gray brows lifted quickly. "What?"

"When you and Mrs. Berrymaple visited the crypt."

"Oh, well, let me see." Mr. Turner flipped the pages of his diary, which had been open on his desk. A thick finger rang down a column and paused on a specific entry. "Here it is. Friday, April eighteenth, two in the afternoon."

"Did you notice anything of interest?" Haley asked. "Anything that seemed out of place or maybe something that you thought would be there that wasn't?"

"Well . . ." His finger moved to his lips. "I dunno. The coffins are sealed behind a brick wall. No stealing one of those, I'll tell you. Plenty of dust. Perhaps that was unexpected."

"Really?" Detective Brock said. "I would think dust was a given."

"Well, I guess. I just thought the custodian would keep it cleaner. No offense to the fella. Sure, he's busy enough doing double duty, keeping the lawn mowed and weeds from taking over the cemetery. Those headstones need to be cared for too." He used his finger to jab at the pile of flyers on his desk. Reading upside down, Haley could make out they were information pamphlets describing the virtues of the society. "We recorded dozens of headstones in danger of deteriorating completely and many more badly weathered. Some are already impossible to read. Poor souls. Forgotten!"

"Thank you for your time," Detective Brock said suddenly, then spun on his heels and marched out.

Haley frowned at the detective's lack of propriety. She held her hand out to Mr. Turner, and the man gripped it with his thick palm.

"Thank you, Mr. Turner. Mrs. Berrymaple is my housekeeper."

"Oh, you're *that* Dr. Higgins! Yes, she speaks very highly of you."

"I'm fond of her as well. Thanks again for the good work you and your society are doing."

Haley was surprised to find that Detective Brock had waited for her. The brim of his hat was pulled down, his arms folded, and his finger rested on his chin.

"What's eating you?" she asked.

"This case is so particular. If we bothered your housekeeper, I suspect she'd have nothing more to add. Same with the groundskeeper. But someone must've seen something. The bones didn't walk into the crypt by themselves."

"How did the perpetrator gain access to the crypt?" Haley said. "He, or she, must've had a key."

Detective Brock nodded slowly. "Manfred Cole would have a key. At the moment, he's the only one we know who could've got inside the crypt.

"Keys can be cut and duplicated," Haley said. "The question is, how securely is the key kept when not in use."

"I suppose we won't know until we ask." Detective Brock stuffed his fists into his jacket pockets. "It may be a fool's errand, so I don't blame you if you'd rather be elsewhere."

"No, I'm quite interested in hearing what Mr. Cole has to say."

THEY FOUND Manfred Cole standing on a walkway between the church and the cemetery, recognizable by his gray overalls, the ring of keys hanging from his belt, and the fact that he was leaning on a hoe. He was talking to a younger man who shared his facial features. He frowned at the intrusion as Haley and Detective Brock approached.

"See ya later, Pa," the younger man said before hurrying away.

"We didn't mean to interrupt," Haley said with a nod to the young man as he disappeared around the corner of the church.

"It's no trouble," Mr. Cole said. "He's a delivery man. Folks hire him to drop off their donations for the rummage sale. There's one every month or so. It helps folks out in these hard times, ya know? Now, how may I help you?"

Detective Brock made introductions and asked how someone would access the crypt.

"Well, you'd need a key."

"And who keeps those," Detective Brock asked. "You?"

Mr. Cole jiggled the clip of keys hanging on a ring from a belt loop. "There's the key I got on my key ring, and then there's the spare key."

"Where's the spare key kept?" Detective Brock asked.

"Oh, in the church. The minister has it in his office."

The minister couldn't be found, but his secretary was happy to help again. "Do a mighty fine work in this city," he said. "Crime is gone up; we see evidence of it all the time, and this atrocity in the crypt is a case in point. Allow me to accompany you?"

Haley and the detective followed the man downstairs to the crypt. He had some trouble releasing the lock. "It's rusted a bit. Oh, here," he added as the lock sprung open. "Would you like me to get you an oil lamp?"

"Not necessary," Detective Brock said. "We have flashlights." He produced his from his inner coat pocket, and Haley retrieved hers from her purse. Together, their lights didn't provide nearly the light of the oil lamps but were enough to guide them safely down the stone steps.

Haley inhaled deeply before descending.

"I'm not sure what we'll find that we haven't already found," Detective Brock said.

Haley busied her mind with the names on the crypts, remembering one that stood out. "Oakes."

"What?"

"It rings a bell. Yes. I remember now. A man called Oakes went missing last year. I never heard if he was ever found."

"A coincidence?"

"I hope not," Haley returned. "The General's wife, Mary Oakes, is buried here too." She wiped the dust off the plate. "She died in 1801. He, in 1783, right at the end of the war, sadly. Only had one son, Jonathan Junior."

The detective had the beam of his flashlight resting at Haley's feet, which weren't what anyone would call dainty. Her brothers teased her about their large size, calling them clodhoppers.

"Detective. Do you mind?"

"Oh, sorry. But I believe you're standing on the very spot where the bones were laid out."

Haley stepped back. "Is it possible the killer purposely set the bones in front of the bricked-up door to the Oakes family vault?"

"It's worth investigating." Detective Brock headed for the steps, and Haley rushed in behind him, eager to get to open air.

"I'll speak to Samantha," Haley said. "See what she can find out."

Detective Brock smirked. "I might as well give my men the day off then."

"Not at all," Haley added quickly. "The more the merrier, right? We'll share if we find anything."

"I know, Dr. Higgins. I see a lot of back-scratching in our future."

Haley said her goodbyes and then caught a taxi to the morgue, her thoughts on the Oakes connection.

If the victim was the missing Oakes man, it was possible he could've been General and Mary Oakes' great-great-grandson. Surely, there had to be other Oakes descendants, but if so, why had the search for the missing man been seemingly dropped?

CHAPTER SEVEN

"The eggs are ready." Mrs. Berrymaple turned off the gas flame beneath the cast-iron pan. The housekeeper was a spry lady in her sixties—Samantha thought regularly tackling four flights of stairs helped. The woman kept her salt-and-pepper hair in a tidy bun and wore a clean white apron. "Fried just how you like them," Mrs. Berrymaple added.

"Thank you, Mrs. Berrymaple," Samantha said as the woman slid two eggs onto her plate and one onto Talia's. The eggs were followed by a slice of lightly buttered toast from the new two-sided toaster Haley had bought. Many folks struggled to put food on the table, and Samantha refused to indulge in anything extravagant, including extra butter. It wasn't too long before that she'd struggled to put food on the table for Talia and her late mother-in-law when they lived in the tenements. And that was before the hardships brought on by the current depression.

Talia suddenly stiffened and stretched her neck as if she remembered something. "Bernice Hamilton says proper young ladies sit up straight when they eat."

Samantha considered her daughter with curiosity. "Who is Bernice Hamilton?"

"Mom. Bernice Hamilton is my best friend."

"How come I haven't heard you talk about her before?" Samantha asked.

Talia lifted her small shoulder. "Bernice Hamilton is new, from California. Everyone wants to be her best friend, and she picked me!"

Samantha wasn't sure if this was a good thing, but she hadn't seen Talia excited about anything or anyone in a long time. Losing her father and grandmother in the same year had taken the wind out of the little girl.

Looking rested and ready to tackle the day, Haley wore a cotton pantsuit. She'd taken to this new trend for women, wearing pants instead of skirts. Samantha hadn't picked up on it yet. Maybe it was a topic to tackle in the ladies' pages. "Are Pants Good or Bad for Women?" Haley poured herself a cup of black coffee from the pot on the stove, then joined them at the kitchen table.

The kitchen was Samantha's favorite room. It had white walls, sage-green cabinets, a cozy wooden table, and a chair set. Along with the gas oven was the 1927 General Electric "Monitor Top" refrigerator. Newer models had been on the market since then, but Haley and, more importantly, Mrs. Berrymaple seemed satisfied with this one. Samantha was just happy to live somewhere with any refrigeration since many folks still made do with iceboxes.

Under the table, a furry presence rubbed against her leg. "Mr. Midnight?" Peeking down at the dark-as-night cat, she caught sight of his long tail and single back leg. The poor three-legged thing had come to live in Haley's apartment, having mysteriously appeared at the fire escape near the kitchen window one stormy night. She gave Talia a side-eye. "Are you feeding the cat your breakfast?"

"I'm sharing, Mom. You told me I should be a sharing girl."

"You don't have to share with Mr. Midnight. Mrs.

Berrymaple feeds him well enough. I think he's getting fat."

Talia protested. "No, he's not."

Haley had the morning paper opened beside her. "Nothing about King's Chapel."

"I should hope not," Samantha said. "Though, I'm surprised. The guys all jumped at some tip that came in from their contacts. I thought one of them might've gotten a tip. Mr. August thought the mayor was up to something, so it must have been that."

"He was. He's preparing his campaign. Daniel Irwin has declared his intention to run against him."

"Interesting."

Mrs. Berrymaple frowned. "Why would King's Chapel be in the news?"

Samantha caught Haley's eye before Haley shrugged.

"I can't say," Haley answered. "Has there been talk about King's Chapel? By the ladies in the society?"

"Oh, it's not just ladies, Dr. Higgins. Some men as well. We talked about the chapel and the burying grounds. They're both a big part of the history of Boston; the city being a hotbed in both the Revolutionary and Civil Wars."

"You seem to know quite a lot about American history," Samantha said. "For a Canadian."

"I dare say Canadians know more about American history than Americans do about Canada. For example, did you know Canada's contribution to the Great War was disproportionate to its population size? Nearly seven percent of Canadians took part. Or that Banff National Park in Alberta is the third oldest national park in the world. I find any kind of history fascinating." She smiled. "If only we'd learn from it."

Haley pushed away from the table. "I'm off to work." She paused by Talia's chair and patted her shoulder. "Have fun at school today."

"Thanks, Auntie Haley. I will. Bernice Hamilton says she's bringing cookies to share with me."

Samantha shared a look with Haley and shrugged.

Haley smiled at Talia. "Do people ever call Bernice Hamilton, Bernice? Without her last name?"

Talia's round blue eyes turned up as she considered the question, then settled back on Haley. "Nope. She's Bernice Hamilton. Two words."

As she did every morning, Samantha walked her daughter to her private school—funded by Haley—before catching the bus to her work on Water Street.

The street view of the building that housed *The Boston Daily Record* was much like many other Boston city buildings. Red brick, flat facade three stories high. Samantha caught sight of her reflection in the ground-floor window that looked into the receptionist area. She frowned. Somehow, she felt older than her twenty-eight years, and now she feared she was starting to look it too.

No time for vanity or self-criticism. Everything she did now and forever was for her daughter, including this job. It didn't matter if she didn't feel like it, or didn't feel qualified, or any other thing that would make her want to turn around, go home, and crawl into bed, including all the testosterone she was about to face in the pen.

She greeted the receptionist, a quiet young man going to night school to study journalism, then pulled on the banister and went up the steps. She inhaled, put her shoulders back, and entered the pen with a cheery hello.

"Aren't you little Miss Sunshine," Fred said with a sneer.

"Good morning to you too, Fred."

Johnny's brows lifted. "You look like the bird who got the worm, Sam. Fess up."

"Nothin' to confess, Johnny." Samantha put her

hat and purse in the desk drawer then stared across the room at Johnny. "But maybe you do? What was the great exodus yesterday?"

"Ah, all smoke, no fire." Johnny leaned back in his chair and put his feet up on his desk. "Mayor's big announcement amounted to a hill of beans. Irwin's decision to run wasn't exactly a big secret."

"Golly. Well, better luck next time." Samantha settled into her chair. "Say, what do you know about the Boston Historical Society?"

Fred harrumphed. "Just a bunch of moneyed folks trying to feel better about not having to go to work."

"It's not all moneyed folk," Samantha protested, as Mrs. Berrymaple wouldn't be categorized as rich.

"I don't know, Fred," Johnny said. "These old buildings are like babies. They need special care, or they won't survive for future generations to enjoy."

"Oh, boo-hoo," Fred said. "As if the future generations are gonna care about old buildings. I think they're more worried about where their next meal is comin' from."

Johnny rolled his eyes then addressed Samantha. "Why the sudden interest?"

"No reason. Mrs. Berrymaple has joined it. It might make a good fluff piece for the ladies' section.

I'm going to check out the archives to see if anything's been written about it, y'know, from before I got here."

This seemed to satisfy the men's curiosity as Samantha headed down the stairs to the archive room. They didn't need to know she was actually looking for a missing person, a man in his forties with a deformed spine and a missing fingertip.

CHAPTER EIGHT

The archives were stored in a windowless room on the same level as the printing press, the composition men, and the darkroom. Samantha waved at Simeon "Inky" Issacson, a wiry man with permanently stained fingers, who managed "Composing." He ensured the men creating the copy with a stamp of each letter in its needed position were doing their jobs.

"G'day, Miss Hawke," Inky yelled over the noise of the printing press.

"Hi there, Inky."

The men in the composing room paused at the sound of their boss' voice, their eyes settling on Samantha with a glint of appreciation. Working in the basement, they didn't see a lot of women.

Sam smiled pleasantly and continued her walk, which she knew to be very feminine, especially in her shapely three-quarter-length skirt and two-inch heels. She laughed at Inky's gravelly voice when he shouted at his men. "Git back to work, you lazy crumbs!"

Samantha pulled on a string, turning on a single bulb, its dim light barely reaching the archive room's corner. She coughed at the dust, stirred up from her entry, and blinked until her eyes adjusted. Floor-to-ceiling shelves lined each wall, and several rows ran down the middle of the room. Each shelf was piled high with hard-bound volumes containing copies of every edition of *The Boston Daily Record* ever printed. The volumes were sorted by month and year, and Samantha searched the shelves until she came to 1931. According to Haley, the John Doe had been dead for at least a year, which would take them back to May 1931. Each year had 352 editions of daily papers. It would take her hours to scour through them all.

Thankfully, a card library at the front of the room cross-referenced the articles in each newspaper. Someone, probably Max Owen, read each paper, identified the article, and placed two reference cards per article into the appropriate card file: one for the date the article ran and one for the subject of the article.

Opening the card file labeled *MI*, Samantha searched for the subject *Missing Persons*. The process stirred dark emotions. Her husband, Seth Rosenbaum, had been a missing person for six years. He hadn't been "missing" technically—more like on the lam. But Samantha had spent the whole time waiting, not knowing if he was dead or alive. It turned out he was alive. He'd shown up suddenly, out of the blue, but his life of crime caught up with him. Now, he was six feet under.

Samantha ferreted through the dates until she got to May 01, 1931, then worked backward. The number of missing persons over a year was disconcerting, and even more so because the missing were disproportionately female.

The men reported missing were typically older, having wandered off due to senility, with a few younger men having had alleged breakdowns reported by their doctors, resulting either from the trauma of the Great War or the stock market crash, or from simply giving up on finding work in Boston. Like Seth had been at the time, many of these men were maybe alive and just out of contact with their families.

Oakes.

Samantha paused at the name. Oakes was a prominent Boston family name, or at least it had once been. She'd learned about General John Oakes' Civil War exploits during history class in school. History wasn't interesting to her, at least not back then, so none of the details came to mind. And it might be that this missing man was no relation to General Oakes. His age and the time of the fella's disappearance lined up with what Samantha knew. According to the notations on the card, the article was written on June 17, 1931.

The volume with the June 1931 issues was stored on a high shelf. Samantha used a step stool to pull it down, awkwardly bracing it on one shoulder as she struggled to keep her balance. Letting it fall onto the table, she pulled it under the lightbulb and flipped it open, scanning each page until she found the write-up on the last page.

Benjamin Alan Oakes, 46, has been reported missing by his brother who says it's uncharacteristic of his brother to leave without notifying him or their house staff. Benjamin Oakes is five foot seven, with light brown hair and hazel eyes. Anyone who knows about this man's whereabouts should contact the police.

Using a pencil and notepad left in the archives

room, Samantha scribbled out the announcement word for word. She ripped the page out of the pad, folded it, and slipped it into her pocket. She needed to learn more about this missing man and his family before returning her findings to Haley.

CHAPTER NINE

The Boston Public Library, a two-story limestone building, had been newly built in 1895. The words "Built by the People and Dedicated to the Advancement of Learning" were in large lettering above the row of second-floor arched windows. Samantha loved the smell of books, researching history, and the excitement of discovering important information. Better yet, her good friend Patty Kingston worked as a librarian assistant at the desk. With a long bob pinned up around the ears, clip-on glass earrings, and a flowing dress complete with a broad lace collar, that had been featured in the most recent spring *Vogue* catalog, she didn't look the type to be working here or anywhere.

"Hi, Samantha," Patty said in a loud whisper. Her

bubbly personality didn't fit in with the quiet and subdued library environment. The job had started as a punishment from her rich father, who had the pull to land a woman in a job a man could do. Samantha wondered how long Patty could hold on to this position, even with Daddy's influence.

"Hey Patty, how's it goin'?"

"Good. Hey, you didn't tell me you were working with a new handsome reporter."

Samantha blinked. "I didn't know I was."

"Oh, I see. Trying to keep the fella for yourself, huh?"

"Patty, what are you talkin' about?"

Patty lifted her chin, her eyes bright as she stared at something over Samantha's shoulder. "Him."

Samantha turned, her jaw dropping at the sight of Doug Wallenburg, Wally, walking their way. His glasses hung from his shirt pocket, and Sam realized she hadn't seen Wally without them on his face before.

"Oh, hey, Sam," he said. "Fancy meeting you here."

"It's a public library." Samantha stared at Wally with new eyes. Removed from the pen environment, Wally showed a type of charm and confidence he seemed to check at the door of *The Boston Daily Record.*

"So it is," Wally said. Then to Patty, "Thanks again for your help, Miss Kingston. It's appreciated."

Patty giggled as she pushed a lock of hair behind her ear. "Anything for you, Mr. Wallenburg."

Samantha's gaze darted from Wally's back as he walked across the library's vast lobby and over to Patty's smitten grin.

"Weren't you dating someone?" Samantha said a tad sharply. "A Mike something?"

"Oh, yeah. Mike Williamson. Daddy likes him."

"I thought you did too?"

"He's all right, I guess. Now . . ." She lowered her voice even more. "What can I help you with?"

"What was Mr. Wallenburg looking for?"

Patty raised a thinly plucked brow. "I don't know if I should tell you that."

"Why not? What's it gonna hurt? Besides, what are friends for?"

"Fine, but you owe me." Her eyes flashed with a look of conspiracy. "He said he's doing a story on this history of missing persons in Boston."

Samantha jerked. "Missing persons?"

"That's what he said."

Does Wally know about the bones in the crypt? Have the press been informed? Dang it.

"Any particular missing person?" Samantha asked.

Patty shrugged. "Dunno. He didn't mention any names. Why?"

"Because I'm also doing a story on a missing person."

That got Patty's attention. "A race to the scoop, huh?"

"Seems that way. I'm looking for what you have on Benjamin Oakes and his family tree."

"Oh, I remember that story. Benjamin Oakes went missing. They never found him, did they?"

"I don't think so."

"Give me a minute."

Samantha waited as Patty retrieved the material from the library, her stomach churning. She'd been the first to track this story. It was hers. She had to hurry.

Patty came back with several binders. "If you tell me what you're looking for, I'll help you look."

"Anything about Benjamin Oakes or anyone from his family."

"He has a brother," Patty said. "Pretty sure about that."

"Do you remember his name?"

Patty shook her head. "Nah."

The library kept copies of Boston's newspapers, not just *The Boston Daily Record,* and most of the nation's papers, but Samantha hoped they'd find whatever they were looking for in one of the local rags. As time went on, her nerves grew tauter. She had a sinking feeling she was about to lose the scoop. Then, her focus fell on a short news report in the margins where legal items were recorded.

"Ah, here we are. His name is Albert Oakes," Samantha said. "He's the younger of two brothers, Benjamin being the eldest. Their parents are Lawrence and Ann Oakes. Lawrence is the descendant of General John and Mrs. Mary Oakes, who are interred in the crypt at King's Chapel."

Patty glanced up. "Anything else?"

"Yes, this from early July last year. 'Mr. Albert Oakes, the brother of the man presumed missing,'" Samantha read aloud, "'Mr. Benjamin Oakes, states he received a letter from his brother with a postmark from England. Mr. Albert Oakes has officially closed the missing person case he filed.'"

Patty closed the binder she was reading. "Mystery solved."

Samantha grinned but disagreed with her

friend's conclusion. The bones found in the crypt remained unnamed. But finding unidentified bones in the crypt was a story on its own. She had to get back to the pen and write it up before Wally beat her to it.

She'd ask Haley for forgiveness later.

SAMANTHA NOTICED that all the desks in the pen were occupied when she returned, except for her own. Ignoring the male glances, some of indifference, some of mild interest, and a couple of keen interest—Johnny's and Wally's, to be exact—Samantha removed her hat and summer gloves and put them, along with her purse, into one of her desk drawers.

She'd discreetly added a layer of cherry-red lipstick in the back seat of the taxi and so faced the onlookers with confidence, asking, "Did I miss somethin', fellas?"

Johnny grinned that adorable, crooked grin that made Samantha's knees turn to liquid, and she was glad she was already sitting down.

"Just wonderin' where you got off to, doll." Johnny winked.

"The library," Wally said, pushing his glasses up

along the bridge of his nose. "Did you find what you were looking for?"

"Maybe," Samantha returned coyly. "Did you?"

It was Wally's turn to grin. He removed his glasses and locked eyes with her. "Maybe."

Good Golly, Miss Molly! Samantha suddenly saw what Patty was talking about! How had she missed seeing Wally the dreamboat? Swallowing, she said, "Good. Well, if you boys don't mind, some of us have work to do."

She looked down just before catching a glare pass between Johnny and Wally. She shook her head. Best not to try to figure it out.

Boston Police Make No Bones About a Callout to King's Chapel

Samantha frowned at her catchy headline. Was it too much?

She continued to write about the police being called to a situation at the crypt and the John Doe found there. She left out the details of the condition of the bones and the distinction of the little finger, as per Haley's instructions, but hesitated before pulling the paper from the roller and walking it to Mr. August's office.

Turning her back to the men in the pen, Samantha picked up her black rotary phone receiver, dialed the operator, and asked to be connected to the morgue. Dr. Martin answered.

"Hello, Dr. Martin, this is Miss Hawke," Samantha started. "Would Dr. Higgins be available?"

"Yes, Miss Hawke," came Dr. Martin's voice. "She just stepped in. One moment."

Samantha snuck a peek over her shoulder as she waited. She felt mildly disconcerted to find both Johnny and Wally watching.

"Samantha?"

Sam lowered her voice. "Hey, Haley. Look, I know you asked me to hold on the crypt story, but I think news of it might have leaked. I want to run the story."

"Yes, I think you should. Have you learned anything?"

"The body doesn't belong to Benjamin Oakes."

"Are you sure? Because, after another look today, we've learned that the bones were placed in front of the vault belonging to a General John Oakes and his wife Mary."

"Interesting," Samantha conceded. "But I found a write-up in a local paper where the brother, Albert, closed the case after getting a letter from his brother, postmarked from England."

"Hmm. A strange coincidence, then. It doesn't sound like your story will be of great length."

"No. Just that a body was found there, and the identity unknown."

"No mention of the—"

"The finger. I know. Thanks, Haley. You can read it in the morning paper."

After hanging up the telephone, Samantha made a few changes to her piece, then, giving the men who glanced up at her a smug smile, walked it over to the editor's office, passing the picture of Abraham Lincoln as she went.

Archie August looked up at her over the rims of his spectacles, then grabbed the page. "What's this?"

"New bones found at the King's Chapel crypt, sir."

Mr. August flipped open the cigar box on his desk and dug a cigar out with fat fingers. "Wallenburg beat you to it."

Samantha's heart dropped to her feet. "What?"

Snipping the tip of the cigar, he nodded. "The story's already downstairs."

"But . . ." Blasted man! How did he know? Haley said the precinct was tight-lipped, but obviously someone had tipped him off. That was why he'd been searching for missing persons in the library.

She snatched her page off the editor's desk. "Sorry to bother you, sir."

"Hawke, you got scooped. It's all part of the game."

Samantha pinched her lips tight, not trusting the words that threatened to burst out. She kept her gaze averted when she marched back to her desk. It was time to pick up her daughter from school, and Sam was more than ready to leave this lot to it.

"Everything okay, doll?" Johnny said with that blasted perpetual smirk.

"Just fine, Johnny." She couldn't stop herself from glaring at Wally. He mouthed back, "Sorry."

"Are you really?" she returned aloud.

Wally shrugged. "Just doin' my job."

Samantha sighed. He was right. A race to the story was the way things worked. She couldn't fault him for unfair play.

"And I'm doing mine," she quipped lamely as she attached her hat and donned her summer gloves.

"Hey," Johnny said with a glint of confusion. "Am I missing something here?"

Samantha stared back. "If you are, you can read about it in the morning edition."

CHAPTER TEN

$\mathcal{A}$fter a frustrating day's work, Samantha looked forward to a quiet evening home with her daughter, but when she walked through the door of the Grove Street fourth-floor apartment she shared with Haley, Talia greeted her in tears.

Samantha pulled her little girl into her arms. "What's the matter?"

"It's Bernice Hamilton. She says I'm not her best friend anymore."

"Oh no." Samantha pulled back and stared into her daughter's watery, blue eyes. "Why not?"

"She likes Sarah better."

"My poor girl," Samantha said with feeling. "Your first heartbreak." Samantha's heart pinched. If only she could spare her darling child the aches and pains the world would present. Rejection, betrayal—the plethora of injustices flung her way simply because she was a female—these were things Samantha couldn't protect her daughter from. She could only give her the skills to deal with them gracefully.

She took Talia's hand and led her to the kitchen. "Let's see if Mrs. Berrymaple has any cookies. Then we'll see what you can do about Bernice Hamilton."

Talia gulped back a sob. "But won't that ruin my appetite?"

Samantha smiled. "It's allowed on special occasions."

The kitchen smelled of fried chicken.

Mrs. Berrymaple stirred gravy in a cast-iron pan using a long-handled wooden spoon. "Oh, hello," she said when she spotted Sam and Talia walk in. Her stirring paused when her gaze landed on Talia's tearstained face. "Is everything all right?"

"It will be," Samantha said. "Nothing a cookie and a glass of milk can't cure."

"Ah . . ."

As if by magic, Mr. Midnight appeared, hop-hobbling on his three legs to Talia. He rubbed his black fur along her bare shins.

"He can tell you need a hug, Talia," Samantha said. "Animals are very smart that way."

Talia scooped the little cat into her arms and awkwardly carried him to one of the chairs. After she slid on to the chair, she locked the cat on to her lap. "I love you, Mr. Midnight," she said into his soft head. "You're a good friend."

Samantha put a cookie on a plate, poured a glass of milk, and delivered both to the table where her daughter sat.

Talia stared up with round eyes. "Shouldn't we give Mr. Midnight some milk too?"

"I suppose if I'm spoiling you, I should spoil him too."

Samantha ignored the quick look Mrs. Berrymaple shot her way and poured a small amount of milk into the cat's bowl. Mr. Midnight jumped to the floor, immediately lapping it up.

Sitting next to Talia, Samantha inhaled, feeling a little unnerved by her responsibility as a mother. She often wished she had someone to share the ups and downs with, who could step in occasionally to help. Haley was a good support but as an aunt-type, not a parent.

"So, tell me what happened?"

"Me and Bernice Hamilton always shared lunches," Talia said quietly.

Samantha wondered if Bernice Hamilton always

referred to Talia as Talia Rosenbaum. Somehow, she doubted it.

"Just for fun," Talia continued, "she'd give me half her sandwich; I'd give her half mine. We split cookies."

"I see." Samantha took a guess. "But today she didn't?"

Talia shook her head. "Today, she shared with Sarah."

"You know. Maybe you've been spending too much time with Bernice." Samantha purposely dropped the last name, hoping to remove whatever power the double-name habit had over Talia. "Having more than one good friend is not a bad idea. Can you think of other girls in your class you may not know as well as you could?"

Talia dipped the last bit of cookie into her milk and popped it into her mouth. "I dunno."

Samantha resisted telling her not to talk with her mouth full—one battle at a time.

"Talia, you will be disappointed many times in your life, sometimes by situations out of your control and sometimes by people you can't control. The only person you can control is yourself. Even God doesn't try to control you."

Talia wrinkled her nose. "He doesn't?"

"No. He gives us free will. What you control is your own outlook. How you decide to handle life's disappointments. Will you learn from them? Make better choices in the future?" Samantha thought of her own recent disappointment with Wally and how she could've handled it differently. "Someone disappointed me today too."

Talia wiped milk from her lips with her forearm. "Oh?"

"And now it's up to me how I will deal with that. Act sad and do a poor job at work, or act confidently, knowing I'm good at my job. You can act confidently, too, knowing you are a good friend even when your friend isn't good to you."

"What should I do, Mommy?"

"You're going to go to school tomorrow. Be friendly with Bernice, and look for another girl to share your lunch with, okay? Then, when we see each other afterward, I'll tell you how it went with my job, and you can tell me about your new friend."

As if he wanted to be part of the resolution, Mr. Midnight jumped onto Talia's lap again.

"Okay," Talia said, her voice lighter. She held Mr. Midnight tightly as she shimmied off the chair. "Mr. Midnight and I are going to read now."

"Good," Samantha said with a feeling of relief.

Talia is fine. "Now, you have to pretend to have an appetite when Mrs. Berrymaple calls us for supper."

Talia smiled. "Yes, Mom."

"You did a fine job there, Mrs. Rosenbaum," Mrs. Berrymaple said as she placed a cup of tea in front of Samantha. Sam hadn't even noticed the tea kettle whistle blow.

"Thank you," Sam said, "for the encouragement and the tea."

"You're welcome."

"Tell me, Mrs. Berrymaple, you visited the crypt at King's Chapel Burying Ground recently—"

Mrs. Berrymaple gave her a side glance of surprise at the sudden change of topic. "For Boston Historical Society records," she said as she busied herself at the stove.

"I suppose you didn't see anything out of the ordinary?"

"Does this have something to do with your problem at work?"

Samantha admired the housekeeper's perceptivity. "Yes. I got scooped on a story."

"What's the story?"

"It'll be in the morning paper," Samantha said, "but this is the gist. A skeleton was found inside; there were new bones. The death occurred a year or so ago. Haley told me but asked that I hold on to the story until she got word from the detective she works with—"

"Detective Brock?"

"Yes. Detective Brock. But by the time I got the okay, someone else at my paper had already submitted the story."

"Ah. That's too bad," Mrs. Berrymaple said with sincerity. "It's hard to keep news like that under wraps."

"I suppose. My colleague obviously has a contact in the police force who works closely with the new detective. It was naive of me to think I was the only one with an inside source."

"You've got a tough job, Mrs. Rosenbaum, dealing with shady people and bad news all the time. I'm quite happy hanging out with a stove and good food." She raised her wooden spoon in jest. "No back talk."

Haley stared at the kitchen window as she sipped her morning coffee. *How nice for her*, Samantha thought irritably. She'd just read Doug Wallenburg's byline in the morning paper and was on edge.

"He named the victim, Haley:

'The victim is presumed to be Benjamin Oakes, a member of Boston's renowned Oakes family, who had been reported missing a year ago in May.'"

After a huff, she added, "Obviously, he didn't do his homework at the library or even bother to chat with the brother." She paused then glanced at her daughter. "Talia, go wash up."

Haley turned to Samantha, who continued to shoo

her daughter away from the table. "It's unfortunate," she said. "Possibly shoddy reporting by Mr. Wallenburg. However, has anyone actually seen Benjamin Oakes since he was reported missing? Albert Oakes suggested a letter was received by the wayward brother. I'm assuming such a letter wasn't physically included in any of the archives you've viewed."

Samantha sipped her coffee. "Well, no. Is there a reason to doubt his accounting of events?"

"When it comes to murder, everyone is suspected." Haley rinsed out her cup and placed it on the drying rack. "Especially close family."

"What should we do now?" Samantha asked as she cleared her own and Talia's dishes.

"Go back to work," Haley said. "As usual. And let the police do their jobs as well."

Samantha's jaw dropped. "Okay, who are you, and what have you done with my curious friend Haley Higgins?"

Haley laughed. "All right. What do you know about Albert Oakes?"

"I'm glad you asked," Samantha said. "I took it upon myself to do a little investigating on Mr. Albert as well. It helps to be connected with someone good at her job at the library."

"Indeed." Haley pulled up a chair. "Don't keep me in suspense."

Samantha joined her and told what she'd learned about Albert and Benjamin Oakes and their parents. "They're direct descendants of General John and Mrs. Mary Oakes."

"Interesting," Haley said. "Anything else?"

"The Oakes family was once very prominent in Massachusetts, much because of the General's heroic track record in the Civil War and because his wife Mary, née Periwinkle, came with money. She and the general only had one son, and from his line only a few descendants, until we're left with Albert."

"And possibly Benjamin," Haley added. "I actually haven't heard of this Oakes family and was surprised by all the references to it being a line of prominence. It makes more sense now. Does Albert hold down a job?"

"Professor at Harvard. Sciences. Interestingly, his brother Benjamin taught history there too. Apparently, the Oakes family has long supported the university, among other things. You'll find the Oakes family name on organizations, and they run a family foundation. It turns out that Harvard's presidency is opening up. I saw the list of professors wanting a shot at the top job."

"Let me guess. Albert Oakes is on the list."

"Yup."

"Sounds like Albert Oakes might be an interesting person to meet," Haley said as she got to her feet. "Field trip?"

"Absolutely." Samantha moved to the telephone hanging on the kitchen wall. "I just have to let Mr. August know I'm following up on a lead and will be late to work."

Haley headed to her home office to collect her things. "We can drop Talia off at school on our way."

The Oakes estate was impressive. A mix of brick and stone, the three-story structure had elaborate detailing, decorative brickwork around the windows and doors, and a steeply pitched roof. The grounds were generous with well-maintained gardens.

The doorbell gong rang out like a gothic funeral dirge, and the door was soon opened by a butler wearing a pressed, single-breasted coat over a starched white shirt and striped pants. Haley was used to seeing men in this service position in England, but she didn't move in a social circle that hired butlers in America.

Haley began with introductions. "We are hoping to have a word with Professor Oakes. Please offer our regrets for coming without an invitation, but we would be grateful if he'd agree to see us."

The butler bowed and motioned for them to step inside. With a distinct English accent, he said "This way, ladies," then led them through open double doors into the sitting room. The interior was as impressive as the exterior, with a grand entrance, high ceilings showing off new electric chandeliers, and a sweeping staircase flanked by carved wooden banisters. "Please wait here," he said, then left them alone.

Several framed ancestral paintings lined the sitting room walls. Haley noticed a few black-and-white prints of the family business, a big meat-packing plant by the docks with "Lawrence Oakes & Co." written over the gates. One photograph was of a group of workers, men wearing caps and striped aprons, with a man in a suit—Benjamin and Albert's father, perhaps—standing center front. The date embossed in the bottom right corner read 1891.

"The General and Mrs. Oakes." Haley started with the first set of paintings with the subject dressed in mid-18th century styles. She moved on to the next painting, a portrait of a couple. "I presume this is the son and his wife." Each painting continued with a couple styled according to their generation until the last.

"And this must be the last of the Mr. and Mrs. Oakes," Samantha said. "I heard they died in a boating accident."

They turned to the door when Professor Albert Oakes joined them. A man of average height and weight, he had a face that didn't elicit attention. Brown eyes, straight nose, trim eyebrows, cleanly shaven.

"I'm Dr. Haley Higgins, Boston's chief medical examiner—"

"Oh, I've heard of you," Albert said, cutting her off. "A woman pathologist. Interesting."

"Yes, I suppose it is," Haley said without smiling. "And this is Samantha Hawke, a *woman* journalist." Haley added the adjective to prevent the professor from stating the obvious again. "Would you mind if we asked you a couple of questions?"

"I'm a slave to curiosity, Doctor." He waved for them to sit down. "You've come some distance out of your way on the chance you'd find me at home. Serendipitous, really, as I'm usually found at the links on a sunny day like today."

"What makes this sunny day different?" Samantha asked. "Why aren't you golfing?"

"Something else has come up."

"This is a spectacular house, Professor," Haley said. "Quite the family tree lining the walls of this room."

Albert sighed. "The family was once a force to be reckoned with. Over the course of generations, well, it's come down to just my brother and me."

"Both of you are quite accomplished," Haley said. "Two professors at Harvard and running a family business on the side."

"Our education was thanks to our father, who worked hard and built up the meat plant." He added grimly, "It was never his intention that we would be left to run it. Now, what do you want to know? I have five minutes to spare."

"We'll be quick," Samantha said.

"I think I can guess why you're here." Albert tented his fingers as he stared from his position on one of the armchairs. "I read the morning papers. I have a mind to sue *The Boston Daily Record*. I've already called to demand a retraction."

"You've spoken to your brother recently, then?" Samantha asked.

"No. Look, Mrs. Hawke—"

"Miss Hawke."

"Miss Hawke. Not all siblings are close. My

brother and I are not. Never were. He left to do research in England. I've received a single missive that let me know he'd arrived. That is all."

"And that was just over a year ago?" Haley asked.

Albert nodded deeply. "About that."

Haley pressed on. "Your ancestors are among the privileged few to be buried in the crypt at King's Chapel Burying Ground."

"So?" Albert rose. "Not that my family, or where any of them is buried, is any of your business. And I can assure you my brother is alive and well." As he tugged on the lapels of his blazer, Haley noticed a slight tremor in his hand. Did their questions make him nervous, or was he in the early stages of a neurological problem?

"Now," the professor continued, "if you don't mind, I have a busy day ahead."

Standing as well, Haley offered her thanks. "Have a great day, Professor."

He nodded. "I'll have Ellsworth show you out."

As good butlers do, the butler appeared out of nowhere and guided them to the front door.

"Friendly folks," Samantha said cheekily as they stepped back outside. "I feel we just wasted the morning."

"Possibly," Haley said. "But I'm glad to put a face to a name."

AFTER DROPPING Samantha off at *The Boston Daily Record*, Haley stopped at the police station on her way to the morgue. When she walked into his office, Detective Brock smiled warmly. "Dr. Higgins. Always a pleasure. Have a seat."

"Thank you, Detective," Haley said, taking the chair. "I imagine you saw the story in *The Boston Daily Record* today?"

"I did. I've been on the telephone with the editor too. I was relieved to see Miss Hawke didn't write the story."

"No. She was just as surprised as the rest of us. I'm assuming a retraction is coming?"

"I've been reassured, yes." Detective Brock crossed one long leg over the other. "I doubt any real harm's been done except to give the killer a good laugh."

"Samantha and I went to see Benjamin Oakes's brother, Albert. He's a professor at Harvard. His brother was, too, before he left for England."

"Yes, we know," Detective Brock said. "Seems the

Oakes connection is a bust. But we've been busy around here, too, chasing other leads."

"Anything of promise?"

Detective Brock shrugged. "Without an identity for the victim, it's nearly impossible to find who would have a motive to kill. No other reported missing persons seem to match our dead body. Fact is, not all murders are solved."

"This one feels personal, though," Haley said. "Keeping the victim until only the bones remained and then purposely placing them in a historical monument."

"He or she does appear to have a bone to pick."

Haley smirked. "Very funny."

"But to your point. There are only four persons with recent access to the crypt."

"Four? There's the groundskeeper Mr. Cole, Mr. Turner, and Mrs. Berrymaple from the historical society. Who's the fourth?"

"Daniel Irwin."

Haley raised a brow. "The councilman?"

"The one and the same."

"Why was he in the crypt?"

"Mr. Cole didn't know."

"I'm surprised he didn't mention Mr. Irwin when we spoke to him."

"He called this morning. Said it slipped his mind. Was sure it would mean nothing to our investigation, but he wanted to be thorough."

"Rather convenient," Haley said. "I'd like to think one of these three men holds the key to our mysterious victim."

"I have the same hope," Detective Brock said. "Which is why I've been digging into their backgrounds."

"Did you find anything of note?"

"I did, Doctor, I did. Mr. Cole's family served the Oakes family until this last generation. Mr. Cole's father worked for the Oakes family as a groundskeeper."

"Another interesting coincidence," Haley said. "I wonder why this Mr. Cole left the mansion for the church?"

"Maybe there was a falling out," Detective Brock said, "or maybe there was no reason. Mr. Turner's history isn't squeaky clean either. Ben Oakes promised to support the society financially but then reneged. Mr. Turner made public threats. Of course, we made these inquiries regarding Ben Oakes when we thought he was the victim."

"Right. And what about Daniel Irwin?"

Detective Brock chuckled. "Ben Oakes was

running against Irwin for a position on the city council and was favored to win."

"Let me guess," Haley said. "Benjamin went 'missing' just before the councilman election, giving Mr. Irwin the seat."

"Correct." Detective Brock fidgeted, tapping his pencil on his notepad. "I'm eager to hear from Scotland Yard."

"You've notified Scotland Yard?" Haley said.

"I think it prudent we track down this Benjamin Oakes and corroborate the brother's story. I want to ensure Ben is indeed living in England somewhere." Detective Brock pushed away from his desk. "In the meantime, paying Mr. Irwin a visit wouldn't hurt."

When Samantha arrived at the offices of *The Boston Daily Record*, the men in the pen were in a heated debate.

Fred Hall smirked. "Mud on your face, Wally?"

"Shut your trap, Hall," Wally spat.

"August is going to print a retraction," Johnny said more amiably.

"Over my dead body," Wally muttered.

"With the mood August is in, that might be exactly how it's going to go down," Johnny said with a sneer. "But look, It's not the end of the world. We've all jumped the gun on occasion."

"I didn't jump the gun, and I'm not retracting," Wally said. "Unless Albert Oakes provides definitive proof, it's his word against mine."

"Do you have evidence that the body found at the crypt is definitely Benjamin Oakes?" Johnny asked. "Or else I call your story shoddy reporting."

Wally's cheeks burned red. "It's not shoddy reporting! It lines up with the missing persons' files."

"How do you know that?" Samantha asked. The room quieted as if just noticing she'd arrived. "How do you know that?" she repeated, though she knew the answer. Wally had a contact with the police close to the case.

Wally smiled at her. "I've got my sources, sweetheart."

"And I got mine," Samantha answered as she settled in at her desk. "Thanks for nothing, Wally."

"What?" Wally returned. "Why are you all in a lather?"

"You scooped my story, and then you messed it up."

Wally harrumphed. "What made it your story?"

"Never mind."

"Hey, hey," Johnny said, putting his hand up like a stop sign. "We're all on the same team here."

"That's a joke, Johnny," Samantha returned. "Everyone here knows I'm on my own."

"Not true, doll. I'm on your side."

Samantha inhaled slowly. She wished he was on

her side in more ways than one. *Think of his gal pal.* Johnny was a coworker, nothing more. "I don't think Wally should retract."

"See?" Wally said triumphantly. "Finally, someone with some sense."

"At least not yet," Samantha amended. "It doesn't hurt to wait a day to see if another name becomes linked with the victim. Aside from that letter his brother claims to have but can't or won't produce, no one has heard from Benjamin Oakes to prove without a doubt that he is still alive."

Johnny stored a pencil above his ear. "I'll put out a few feelers, see what I can learn about good ol' Ben."

Wally slugged the last of his coffee, then hopped up from his desk toward the men's room. Once he was out of earshot, Johnny said, "I'd keep things friendly with Wally."

Samantha shot him a look. "I'm friendly with everyone."

"And that's the kind of friendly I'm talkin' about, doll."

"Why do you care how friendly I am with anyone, Johnny? How's the gal pal?"

Johnny frowned. "I'm just sayin' there's more to Wally than what meets the eye. Be careful."

Samantha's chest burned with fury. What business did Johnny have, trying to influence her love life? She didn't even have a love life, but Johnny didn't need to know that either. *Just who does he think he is?*

When the telephone on Wally's desk rang, Samantha didn't think twice before jumping up to answer it, glaring at Johnny, daring him to stop her. She picked up the receiver. "Doug Wallenburg's desk."

"Uh, Samantha?"

Samantha blinked at the sound of the familiar voice. "Tom?" She and Officer Tom Bell had once had a thing going. A light flirtation that went nowhere and a brief period when she'd considered him her police contact. The truth registered. "You're *Wally's* contact now?"

"I didn't know you were answering Mr. Wallenburg's desk telephone, Miss Hawke. Slow news day?"

"Just doing a fellow journalist a favor, Officer Bell. Would you like me to take a message?"

"Nah. I'll call back later."

"I'll tell him that. Goodbye."

Samantha hung up before any more such pleasantries could be exchanged. She kept her gaze averted from Johnny's ceaseless watching and returned to her desk. Since part of her agreement with Mr. August was to keep up with the ladies' pages in exchange for the freedom to follow up on other stories, she turned her attention to the next column she needed to write. She kept a notebook to record ideas, everything from fashion to housekeeping, gardening, recipes, and social events. Some articles were meant to shine a light on the difficult times women found themselves in and offer tips on how to make life easier, and other articles were meant to provide a mental escape, written as if a depression wasn't going on at all.

Samantha felt it was time for the latter and scoured her list of ideas: Free things to do with young families during tough times. Yes. Feeding ducks at the Common, reading at the public library, dipping toes in the cool waters of the Charles River . . .

Looking to keep your young'un occupied while on a budget? Here are five things you can do with your family that won't cost you a penny!

She sensed someone standing behind her before being proved right by the sound of a man lightly clearing his throat. She turned to see Wally there.

"Mr. Wallenburg?"

"Wally, please, Sam."

"Wally. Do you need something?"

Wally stepped closer, effectively blocking Johnny's view of Samantha's desk with his back. Lowering his voice, he said, "I was wondering if you wanted to get lunch someday. Ya know, exchange notes?"

Samantha smiled as she glanced around the man and saw Johnny staring hard. "A date?" she asked loudly. Then more softly. "Or business only?"

He leaned casually against her desk, his arms folded over his chest, then smiled in return. "Whichever you prefer."

Wally's change of position put Johnny in full view. She was about to gently decline Wally's offer when Johnny slowly shook his head.

"I'll think about it, Wally," she said.

He pushed himself from her desk. "I'll take that."

"Oh, by the way, your phone rang while you were out. I hope you don't mind that I answered it for you. Officer Bell says he'll call you back."

Wally stiffened, then relaxed. "Thanks, Sam."

COUNCILMAN IRWIN WAS FOUND at the city hall, where he occupied a small office. Mr. Irwin was a sturdy-looking man with thick arms and strong shoulders, someone who could take care of himself in a brawl.

The detective jumped right in. "I'm Detective Brock, and this is Dr. Higgins. We'd like to ask you a few questions about Benjamin Oakes."

The councilman's eyes narrowed, shifting between Haley and Detective Brock. He motioned to the empty chairs in front of his desk. "Have a seat, please."

Haley wondered at Detective Brock's inclination to abruptness and brashness—did he do it intentionally to unnerve his suspects, or was he actually unaware of his apparent idiosyncrasies?

"Right," Detective Brock said as he lowered himself into the chair, his long legs bending sharply. He sat his dented hat on his pointy knees. "I understand Mr. Oakes was your nemesis, Mr. Irwin."

Mr. Irwin chuckled uncomfortably. "I'd say the word 'nemesis' is a little strong. He was my competitor, Detective. Nothing more sinister than that."

"Yet, he was the favored candidate in your race, was he not?"

Shrugging a shoulder, Mr. Irwin said, "According to some."

Detective Brock persisted. "How was it that you overcame your odds?"

Leaning back in his chair, Councilman Irwin threaded his fingers together then said, "Why don't you tell me what this is about, Detective?" His eyes darted to Haley. "And why have you brought a lady doctor along with you?"

"I'm Boston's chief medical examiner," Haley said. "As a councilman, you must've heard of me."

"Ah, yes, of course." Mr. Irwin glanced at her with a look of suspicion. "There was much debate about filling that position when Dr. Guthrie retired. You're lucky you were in good graces with the mayor."

"I like to think my experience and qualifications had something to do with it," Haley said stiffly.

"Yeah, sure."

"We've discovered a body," Detective Brock said, "and decomposition has made identification difficult. I've asked Dr. Higgins to counsel the police on the case."

"Okay. So, what does that have to do with me and Oakes?"

"We are trying to eliminate beyond doubt the possibility that this body belongs to Mr. Oakes," Detective Brock said. "Certain attributes Dr. Higgins identified were compared with the file of missing persons we have at the precinct."

"I see," Mr. Irwin said. "And you're here because

you think I had something to do with Ben Oakes's disappearance."

"We find it curious, that you had reason to visit the crypt at King's Chapel recently," Detective Brock said. "Would you mind sharing why you were there?"

Mr. Irwin shrugged. "Curiosity. The Boston Historical Society has suggested the possibility of making tours available to the public, to help raise funds." The man shook his head. "I can't see how anyone would pay to step into a cellar and stare at a brick wall. I opposed the idea."

"When was the last time you saw Mr. Oakes?" Detective Brock asked.

Mr. Irwin scowled then, looked as if he were about to protest, then let out a long breath in resignation. Flipping backward through the pages of his appointment book, which lay open on the top of his desk, he found the date he was looking for and jabbed it with his finger.

"Last year, Friday, April the third. We had a scheduled debate the next day, but he didn't show."

Haley made a mental note of the date. It lined up with the time of death she'd projected. "What type of person is Mr. Oakes?" she asked.

Mr. Irwin scoffed. "What does that have to do with anything?"

"It allows us to profile the victim," Detective Brock said. "Which helps with understanding possible motive."

"He is a headstrong, belligerent, egotistical narcissist. He wanted to win, not to serve the people but to serve himself."

"And yet, the people seemed to want him over you," Haley said.

"That's because he is a charming, beguiling snake. The ultimate liar."

"You have strong feelings against the man," Detective Brock said.

"Yeah, well, I'm not the only one. His own brother despises him. Look," Mr. Irwin leaned in, propping his elbows on his desk, "I don't like the man, but I didn't kill him." Leaning back, he continued, "If someone did, they did me a favor. Now, if you don't mind, I have a meeting to prepare for."

CHAPTER THIRTEEN

The next morning at the morgue, Haley reviewed Dr. Martin's notes about the mystery bones. The victim had not only had a mishap sometime in his life that caused the loss of his fingertip, but he also suffered from what seemed to be spinal tuberculosis, also known as Pott's disease. It wasn't so advanced to be obvious to the casual observer, but it would have definitely caused chronic back discomfort.

The door to the morgue opened, and Haley caught sight of Detective Brock's dented fedora before he pulled back into the corridor and knocked on the still-ajar door.

"Dr. Higgins?"

Haley moved to her office door and beckoned, "Come in, Detective."

The detective removed his hat, holding it with long fingers as his arm hung low. "Sorry for dropping in unannounced." His tall forehead formed worry lines. "Do you have a moment?"

Haley felt a shiver of concern at Detective Brock's furtive behavior. "Certainly. Let's go into my office." She shot Dr. Martin a look before leading the detective behind the glass walls of her office. She sat behind her desk, but he remained standing.

"Detective, please sit. You're making me nervous."

Nodding, the detective pulled the wooden chair a bit further from the desk—to allow for room for his long legs—and sat. "I've got new news on the case."

"I'd love to hear it."

"Yes, well, it turns out that a Mr. Edward Berrymaple once worked as a night watchman at the meatpacking plant the Oakes family own."

Haley's nerves shot out warning signals. "Are you talking about my Mrs. Berrymaple's late husband?"

"I am. According to one of the workers at the plant, there was growing tension between the eldest son Benjamin Oakes and Mr. Berrymaple. Mr. Ben Oakes believed that money was being stolen from the petty cash. He'd accused more than one worker without proof, and eventually, he decided Mr. Berrymaple was the thief, something Mr. Berrymaple vehemently denied. It was during this altercation that Mr. Berrymaple's heart gave out. He died at the plant."

Haley felt the blood drain from her face. "I see."

"Were you aware of these facts about Mr. Berrymaple, Dr. Higgins?"

"I was not. I've only known Mrs. Berrymaple as a widow. I know that she and her husband never had children. Also, she's originally from Canada but has lived in Boston for so long that she considers it home."

"What else do you know about her?"

"She's a terrific cook and baker and wonderful with Samantha's daughter, Talia." Haley pursed her lips as she sharply shook her head. "Detective Brock, you can't seriously be considering Mrs. Berrymaple a suspect?"

"Are you saying I shouldn't? Let's consider the facts. Mrs. Berrymaple, as a member of the Historical Society, has recently visited the crypt where the bones were found. The bones were laid at the base of the Oakes vault. And now we find that her husband worked for the Oakes family and died in their factory."

Haley sighed. "I admit, that's a lot of coincidences. But I have to point out that we don't have confirmation of the body's identity. Regardless, I just can't see it. Mrs. Berrymaple is in her sixties. Hardly the type to go up against a man. And where would she have stored the body until it was nearly skeletal? Not in her apartment. There's a smell to consider."

"Maybe she didn't work alone."

"Who with? Mr. Turner from the historical society? And what would be his motive?"

Detective Brock leaned back in the chair and stretched out a leg. "Well, let me drop another coincidence in your lap. Ben Oakes had promised to make a financial contribution to the historical society, large enough to keep the society afloat for a good many years, then reneged, leaving the society in a lurch."

"Yes, you've mentioned this before," Haley said. "But, I can't see Mr. Turner murdering someone like that, then going to the trouble to hide the body."

"No body, no murder."

"True," Haley said. "Then why suddenly provide a body? It's self-sabotaging."

"That I can't tell ya. Only that when push comes to shove, men and women have been known to do strange and terrible things."

Haley couldn't argue with that. "What is your next move?"

"Well, I'll have to talk to Mrs. Berrymaple and Mr. Turner again."

"I'd like to be with you when you talk to Mrs. Berrymaple," Haley said. If only it were easy to provide an alibi, but the circumstances of this case made that virtually impossible. "Keep in mind, coincidences *do* happen."

"On occasion, yes. I'll be as kind as I can, but I have to do my job. You understand, right?

"Of course, Detective. Shall we go now?"

The detective stood. "That would be best."

Haley felt a strange sense of satisfaction at Detective Brock's barely concealed shortness of breath as they took the stairs to the fourth floor of her Grove Street apartment building.

"I understand now," he huffed, "why you're in such good shape."

Haley held in the smile that threatened. She enjoyed the compliment coming from Detective Brock more than she should. She deflected. "I'd have to say the same for Samantha and Mrs. Berrymaple. Even at her age, she travels up and down these steps daily, often with her arms holding heavy grocery bags."

Her boasting of Mrs. Berrymaple's physical strength and stamina had the opposite of her intended effect.

"Strong for a woman, huh," Detective Brock said. He paused on the landing to settle his breath. "I'm beginning to see that my second-floor apartment is doing me a disservice."

Haley realized in that instant that she didn't know where the detective lived. He had her at a disadvantage on that count, but she certainly wasn't going to ask for his address.

"Which apartment is hers?" he asked.

Haley pointed to the one at the end of the hall.

"And you said she's next door to yours, so you must live here." He pointed to her front door.

"That's correct."

Haley stepped up to her neighbor's door and knocked.

"When was the last time you went into this apartment?" Detective Brock asked.

Haley realized that she'd only ever been inside once, a couple of Christmases back.

"Mrs. Berrymaple comes daily to cook and clean. I don't have a reason to intrude on her privacy when she's off work."

Mrs. Berrymaple opened the door, her eyes rounding in surprise. "Dr. Higgins?"

"Please forgive this intrusion," Haley said. "I'm working with the police on the case of the mysterious bones that showed up at the King's Chapel crypt, and the police need to speak with everyone who has been inside it recently. This is Detective Brock."

Detective Brock removed his crooked hat and nodded politely. "Mrs. Berrymaple. I'm afraid I need a moment of your time."

Mrs. Berrymaple seemed to recover from her shock. Smoothing out her apron, she said, "Do come in. I'll make a pot of tea."

"That won't be necessary," Detective Brock said. "We won't be long."

"Very well."

Mrs. Berrymaple's apartment had a similar look and feel to Haley's, though it was smaller. Haley guessed about half the size. Still, the apartments weren't cheap to buy, and the rent would be higher in this building than in other neighborhoods. Haley assumed that the Berrymaples had done well for themselves during the '20s, as she herself had, and made a smart move to cash in their investments before the crash. And maybe that was the case. Haley never thought it was her business to ask.

But now, knowing what Mr. Berrymaple did for a living, she wondered about their resources. Could he have come into money unethically? If he had, he wouldn't have been alone. Samantha herself had come into money on the death of her husband, who had been a known criminal.

Mrs. Berrymaple sat upright, hands folded on her lap and her ankles crossed. "How can I help?"

Detective Brock cleared his throat. "It's come to our attention, Mrs. Berrymaple, that the Oakes family employed your husband before he passed away."

Mrs. Berrymaple's round eyes darted to Haley, then back to the detective. "That's correct."

"Can you tell me the nature of his employ?" the detective asked.

"He was a night watchman at Lawrence Oakes & Co."

"I'm new to Boston," Detective Brock started, "but isn't that the meatpacking plant down by the docks?"

"That's right," Mrs. Berrymaple confirmed. "Edward's nephew, Nick, works there. Got my husband on."

Mrs. Berrymaple had mentioned her nephew-by-marriage in passing, but Haley had never met the man.

"How long did your husband work at the plant?"

"Not all that long. Maybe two and a half years before—you know." Her frown deepened. "I didn't want him to take the job, but he'd lost money in a bad investment, you see, and wanted to make it back."

"Did he ever lock horns with the Oakes brothers?"

Mrs. Berrymaple's face crumpled in consternation. "I don't understand why you're asking these questions." She faced Haley. "Dr. Higgins?"

"I'm sorry, Mrs. Berrymaple. I know the questions are uncomfortable, but please do your best to answer them."

After a heavy sigh, Mrs. Berrymaple turned back to the detective. "The first couple of years, things were fine. I didn't like him working nights—it upset our schedule as a couple—but I got used to being quiet during the morning and early afternoons while Edward slept. Then we had a few hours together before he left for work, and I went to bed."

"And then . . ." Detective Brock prompted.

"Then Benjamin Oakes accused my Edward of stealing from the petty cash box."

Detective Brock leaned in. "Was he?"

Mrs. Berrymaple stiffened, fire behind her eyes. "Absolutely not! I don't know who had the sticky fingers, but it wasn't my Edward. I would've noticed if we had money at our disposal that couldn't be accounted for by his pay stubs. Mr. Ben had it in his head that Edward could no longer be trusted. Poor Edward's reputation was on the line. 'If a man doesn't have his good name, then he doesn't have anything,' he'd say. But Mr. Albert took Edward's side."

"Despite these accusations, Mr. Berrymaple stayed at the meat plant?" Detective Brock asked.

Mrs. Berrymaple shrugged. "'A job's a job,' Edward said, and in those days like now, they weren't growing on trees."

"What happened on the night of your husband's death?" Detective Brock asked.

Mrs. Berrymaple wrung her hands. "I wanted him to quit his job. I knew Edward had a bad heart. Mr. Ben's slander had kept him from sleep. No job was worth getting sick over. He finally agreed to leave his post and was going to resign that night." Mrs. Berrymaple's bosom rose as she let out another long breath. "He never made it home. I don't know if he had a chance to quit, but Nick said that he'd overheard another argument between Edward and Ben Oakes."

"Do you believe Ben Oakes is responsible for your husband's death?" Detective Brock asked.

Mrs. Berrymaple stared at the detective with a hardened look, an expression Haley had never seen on her housekeeper's face before. "I do, Detective, I do."

"Did you ever meet Mr. Ben Oakes personally?" Haley asked.

Mrs. Berrymaple nodded. "On occasion."

"Do you recall, was Ben Oakes missing the tip of a little finger?"

Mrs. Berrymaple's brow crumpled. "You know, I never saw that, and Edward never mentioned it."

"What about Ben Oakes's gait? Was he slumped over when he walked?"

Shaking her head, Mrs. Berrymaple said, "I never noticed. Though, he was always wearing a heavy coat or vest."

Haley wasn't reassured. Were they wrong about the identity of the John Doe? Was Ben Oakes truly alive and well in England, as Albert had claimed?

Haley snapped to attention when she sensed

Detective Brock getting to his feet. "Thank you for your time, Mrs. Berrymaple," he said. "We can show ourselves out."

"Dr. Higgins," Mrs. Berrymaple started. "Would you mind if I took the evening off? There are left-overs in your refrigerator. I'm feeling exhausted."

"Of course, that's fine," Haley said gently. "We'll chat tomorrow. Try to rest up."

Haley closed Mrs. Berrymaple's door as she entered the hall. She wanted a word with the detec-tive. *What does the nephew, Nick, have to do with anything?*

Then suddenly, she knew.

Unfortunately, Detective Brock was nowhere in sight, having left abruptly as Haley had come to know he was likely to do.

Haley was sure she would meet up with him again soon. She jumped into her DeSoto and headed for the Lawrence Oakes & Co. meatpacking plant.

Samantha was focused on her ladies' article, her fingers stabbing the raised typewriter keys with precision, when Johnny sauntered in.

"So," he started, "I've been doin' a bit of my own diggin.'"

Wally startled. "Whatcha mean? On my story?"

Samantha jumped in. "You mean my story, dontcha, Wally?" They were all newshounds, so it didn't surprise Samantha that they sensed a good story was buried here somewhere. An unidentified skeletal body and a possible missing person. It could be two stories or one. If only Ben Oakes could be found and interrogated.

"Keep your hair on, sweetheart," Wally said with a wink. "It's dog eat dog."

"You're new here, Wally," Johnny said as he lit a cigarette. "This may be a bullpen, but Miss Hawke can pull her own weight."

Samantha couldn't help but smile at Johnny coming to her defense. She added, "We'll see who gets to the finish line first."

Fred Hall blustered, "Can y'all just shut your traps? A man can't even think around here."

"What's to think about, Freddy?" Johnny jested. "Sharkey's up against Schmeling in the championship fight. It's not a difficult puzzle."

Fred Hall grumbled, then turned back to his typewriter, chicken-pecking the keys with thick index fingers.

"So whatcha dig up, Johnny?" Samantha asked.

Johnny's brow arched as he tapped ash into his ashtray. "So, we're sharin' now?"

"It's called collaborating," Samantha said.

"Whatcha got, then?"

"You already know what I got," Samantha shot back.

"Yeah, a whole lot of nothing," Johnny returned with a smirk.

"Which is exactly what I think you got, Milwaukee," Wally said. "A big fat nothing-ball." He turned to Samantha. "He's just tryin' to get us riled up."

Johnny put his feet up on his desk. "I guess you'll never know."

"Never mind him, Sam," Wally said. "Why don't you and me go out for somethin' to eat? You said you'd think about it, remember?"

Samantha batted her lashes. "Business or pleasure?" She was aware that her voice was flirtatious. She was also, sadly, aware she was putting on a show for Johnny.

"Why not both?" Wally said.

"Sam—" Johnny said, giving her a stern look.

Samantha couldn't deny the pleasure she felt at Johnny's concern and worry he'd expressed over her. She could only guess why he thought Wally would be a bad date. Her hope was Johnny's reason came from deeper feelings he had for her. She was about to turn Wally down when a raspy female voice made her turn around. She frowned. Johnny's gal pal, Miss Melrose.

"I was in the neighborhood, honey," Miss Melrose said, heading to Johnny's desk with swaying hips. "Any chance yer free for dinnah?"

Samantha stared wide-eyed at the gal's boldness. A lady didn't do the asking in these situations, though Samantha often wondered why not. Johnny frowned at Miss Melrose then glanced at his watch. "I'm busy, Betty. Maybe later."

Johnny got to his feet and took Miss Melrose by her elbow, ushering her back toward the door and down the steps.

Samantha busied herself by inserting a clean sheet of paper into her typewriter roll, even as she felt her cheeks warm with embarrassment. Why couldn't she let Johnny go? Why was she torturing herself in this way? Once upon a time, Johnny might have been a family man, but he wasn't anymore. He was no good for her. No good.

Johnny whistled as he returned to his seat.

Samantha sat straight, emboldened. "Wally, I'd be happy to join you for dinner."

Johnny's smile fell.

Samantha didn't care. What she did and with whom was none of Johnny Milwaukee's business.

Her heart stammered as she caught sight of the wall clock. She had to leave or she'd be late picking up Talia from school. Mrs. Berrymaple had left a message with the paper's receptionist telling Sam she wasn't feeling well and couldn't collect Talia today. Sam hoped the housekeeper wasn't coming down with anything serious, especially nothing contagious. She grabbed her hat, gloves, and purse.

"See ya later, boys," she said, rushing out of the room.

LAWRENCE OAKES & Co. was a large brick warehouse in South Boston. The advertising billboard near the front entrance was printed in large lettering: PORK, LARD, Tripe, Sausages, Pig's Feet. All cuts of BACON AND HAMS, for home and foreign trade. Also, manufacturers of EXTRA LARD OIL. Then, in smaller letters: Slaughtering and Curing Establishment.

Haley wondered just how much money Mrs. Berrymaple had. Previously, Haley would've considered it none of her business. Not all people with money liked to advertise the fact. Especially when so many suffered without. She assumed Mrs. Berrymaple was well enough off, living in the same stylish apartment building as Haley herself. She worked for Haley and Samantha, not out of necessity but for companionship.

But the way she talked about her husband having to work. Maybe he'd had a good life insurance plan.

Haley entered through the nondescript front entrance in search of the meat plant manager and wasn't the least bit surprised to find Detective Brock already there, speaking with him. He startled when he saw her.

"We could've saved on gas and come together," Haley said.

The detective nodded. "I didn't think a slaughter-house was a place for a lady."

Haley made a face. "I deal with dead bodies. I think I can handle the smell and whatever else you might think could offend my delicate feminine disposition."

Detective Brock tipped his hat. "My apologies. But now that you're here, do you know what we're looking for?"

"A cool place to hide a body for a year?" Haley said.

Detective Brock motioned to the plant manager, a short man with a receding hairline. The nameplate on his office door read Mitchell Cromwell.

"Mr. Cromwell, this is Chief Medical Examiner Dr. Higgins."

The manager's long face tightening with suspicion. "I can't imagine what would bring the police and the medical examiner to our plant."

"We have a few questions about a former employee, Mr. Edward Berrymaple."

"Ed? He had a heart attack about five years ago." The manager shrugged. "I haven't thought about him much since, poor fella."

"We understand that Mr. Berrymaple and his employer, one of his employers, Mr. Benjamin Oakes, didn't get along."

"I suppose you could say that. I really don't know what their beef was about."

"We've heard Mr. Oakes accused Mr. Berrymaple of stealing," Haley said.

"Well, yes, I do recall that."

"But you never saw evidence of theft?" Detective Brock asked.

"Not directly. No. And Mr. Albert Oakes thought it was poppycock."

Haley pushed aside a wayward curl. "Why would Ben Oakes make such a spurious claim about an innocent man?"

"I couldn't say, ma'am."

Detective Brock raised his chin toward the manager. "Did a Nick Berrymaple work here during this time?"

"Yeah, and he still does. A good worker, Nick. Never causes any trouble. We hired his uncle on his recommendation. And everything was good until . . . it wasn't." His gaze locked on something behind Haley and the detective, and he added, "Speak of the devil. Nick? What is it?"

Turning, Haley laid eyes on a man dressed in overalls, who was hurrying in their direction, a look of urgency on his face.

"Mr. Cromwell, ya have to see this." Nick's distressed expression twisted more deeply when his gaze landed on Haley and the detective. "Alone."

"Excuse me," Mr. Cromwell said.

Haley and Detective Brock shared a quick look, then stepped in behind the two men. Whatever it was that a plant worker who worked with dead animals and raw meat every day found disturbing, they wanted to know about it.

Nick Berrymaple led them across the courtyard, a dirt square in the middle of the four encasing brick edifices of the packing plant. The air smelled of burned coal with the putrid scent of burned animal carcasses. The man pointed at an old travel trunk with its lid open in the corner of the courtyard.

Detective Brock, a couple of steps ahead of Haley, looked in the trunk, then jerked back.

"What is it?" Haley asked. She stepped around Detective Brock, who'd been blocking her view.

Inside the large travel trunk was the body of Mr. Turner from the Boston Historical Society. Haley wiped the dust off the nameplate and gasped. The owner of the trunk was Mrs. Edna Berrymaple.

CHAPTER FIFTEEN

Haley retrieved her black doctor's bag from her DeSoto, then stayed with the body while Detective Brock left to use the telephone in the manager's office. She used her time alone with Nick Berrymaple to ask questions.

"Mr. Berrymaple, I'm Dr. Haley Higgins. I employ your aunt."

Nick eyed Haley with appreciation. "*You're* Dr. Higgins?"

"You seem surprised."

"Well, I just imagined you'd be, ya know, older. Like my aunt." Nick averted his gaze. "Poor thing. How did her trunk get involved in this?"

"That's what I'd like to know," Haley said. "Your aunt says you got your uncle a job here, at the plant."

Nick frowned. "I did. Thought I was doin' him a favor at the time."

"She also said you overheard an argument between your uncle and Benjamin Oakes."

"That good-for-nothin'. He had more money than he knew what to do with, yet he had the audacity to accuse Uncle Ed of stealin' from the petty cash. Absurd is what it was. Uncle Ed was as straight as an arrow, as honest as they come. It crushed him to have his name sullied like that."

The conversation was cut short by Detective Brock's return. He held a police-issued Nikon in his hand. "I keep it in my car, just in case," he said at Haley's look. "An ambulance is on its way."

"If you don't need me," Nick Berrymaple said, "I've gotta get back to work."

"I know where to reach you," Detective Brock said with a nod. He took a bunch of photos of the body in the trunk. When he seemed satisfied, Haley asked, "Am I cleared to examine the body?"

"Yes, please do."

The body had been pushed in, back first, with the neck and limbs forced—probably broken—to fit it inside. Had Mr. Turner been a large man, the killer would've had to find another way to transport and conceal the body. There wasn't any sign of petechial hemorrhaging, so he hadn't suffocated while in the trunk. The suit jacket appeared soiled. Haley pulled the lapel away from the shirt, where a large blood-stain was noticeable.

"Detective, would you give me a hand removing the body? I'm afraid he's stiff with rigor." Haley pressed down on the edges of the trunk while the detective pried the body out and set it on the ground. With rigor mortis still in full force, the corpse lay on one side like an enormous fetus in a suit.

Detective Brock snapped more photographs of the empty trunk and the deformed-looking body at his feet. Having got what he wanted, he put the camera aside then asked, "What can you tell me, Doctor?"

The source of the bleeding seemed to be the left side of the man's chest. Haley opened up the shirt. "Appears to be a gunshot wound to the heart. He would've died instantly."

"Time of death?"

"Hard to say at the moment. By the condition of the rigor, which is beginning to soften, I'd guess in the last twelve to twenty-four hours."

"I'll talk to his wife," Detective Brock said. "Find out when she last saw her husband alive." The screeching sound of the ambulance siren announced its arrival. "Is the body ready to be moved, Doctor?"

Haley nodded. Catching movement in her peripheral vision, she turned to focus on the man speaking with the plant manager.

Johnny Milwaukee? His police contact must've taken Detective Brock's call. Samantha was going to be steamed.

Brushing off her wide-leg slacks, Haley headed for the journalist, surprised that Detective Brock hadn't already played interference. He'd disappeared behind the ambulance, probably giving instructions that the driver already knew. Take it to the city morgue.

Haley pushed curls off her face as she called out, "Mr. Milwaukee."

"Oh, hello, Dr. Higgins," Johnny said. He mumbled something to Mr. Cromwell, then walked away from the man, bridging the gap to Haley. "Fancy meeting you here."

"I don't think you're surprised by my presence at all." Haley forced pleasantry. "I would be called to attend when a body is found." She didn't mention she had already been at the scene when it happened. "You being here, on the other hand, and so quickly, is a surprise."

"I guess you could call it serendipity."

"You just happened to be passing by the meat-packing plant, and an ambulance pulled in?"

"Something like that." Johnny looked relaxed and casual, his hat tilted just so and his hands in his pants pockets. "So, I understand you got yourself another homicide. Poor man stuffed into a big ol' trunk."

Haley ground her teeth—*dang plant manager.* Detective Brock hadn't had a chance to give the man a gag order.

"I can neither confirm nor deny."

"Aw, c'mon, dol—"

Haley stopped the man from calling her "doll" with a sharp look. *The audacity!*

He saved himself. "—Doctor. I'm gonna write it up. Better that I have all the facts, right?"

"I agree. You should wait until you have the facts, but I'm afraid you'll get nothing more from me. Good day, Mr. Milwaukee."

THE BODY HAD BEEN DELIVERED by the time Haley arrived at the morgue, Dr. Martin having signed it in.

Dr. Martin set the tray of surgical instruments on

the trolley beside the table. "Is it true he was found at a meat plant?"

"It's true."

"Did he carry identification?"

"I didn't check," Haley said. "Didn't need to. I know who he is. Though the wife needs to make an official identification."

"Yeah?" Dr. Martin went through the motions of checking the suit pockets and dropped loose coins and a set of keys into a bowl.

"His name is William Turner. Retired. He volunteered at the Boston Historical Society."

Dr. Martin paused and stared at Haley. "Didn't I hear that your housekeeper volunteered there as well?"

Haley nodded briefly. "I'm sure it's not connected."

Her words held conviction, but her heart skipped a beat. Grief could do strange things to people—lead normally sound personalities to behave uncharacteristically. "I need to make a call, then I'll help you get started on the autopsy."

Dr. Martin's brow arched. "You want to do it tonight?"

"Do you have something better in mind?" Haley knew it was an unfair comment. Tom Martin was a young man who, perhaps, didn't see himself married to his job. "It's fine if you do. I can manage on my own."

"No, I can stay." He grinned. "No big date planned." Dr. Martin tugged on the deceased man's arm. "He's softened. Enough that we can manage a Y incision. I'll cut off his clothes and get him ready."

Haley stepped into her office, took a long breath, and lowered herself into her chair. It'd been a long day. An ineffective meeting with Albert Oakes, an uncomfortable discussion with Mrs. Berrymaple, a second death that seemed to be connected with the yet unidentified bones found in the crypt, a testy meetup with Mr. Milwaukee, and now an autopsy to perform.

But first, she had to call Samantha. The operator put her through, and Samantha answered on the third ring. "Haley? Is everything all right?"

"Yes. I just wanted to let you know I'll be working late."

"Just me and Talia, huh? Mrs. Berrymaple isn't here either."

"I know. Look, Samantha, we have things to catch up on. There's been another body, Mr. Turner, from the Boston Historical Society."

"Golly. Does Mrs. Berrymaple know?"

Haley hoped not. The only way she would was if . . . "It's complicated. But the thing is, Mr. Milwaukee showed up at the scene—"

"Johnny was there? Wait. Where?"

"At the meat plant. It's a long story."

"So, Johnny's got the scoop."

"Looks like it."

"I'll wait up."

"I'll be a couple of hours, yet."

"That's all right. I promised Talia a game of Snakes and Ladders, and then we'll read *Ozma of Oz* at bedtime. I'll still be up when you get home."

"Sounds good. See you then."

Haley tidied her hair—brushing it off her face and into a tight bun—washed her hands in the morgue sink, and tied on a clean white apron. She marveled at the hospital laundry and how the women worked miracles, getting bloodstains out and then returning everything a bright white.

Dr. Martin had worked the corpse's arms and legs into milder angles, a sheet draped over the bottom half of the body. The man's chest was exposed with a bright red contusion where the bullet had entered.

"No bullet?" Dr. Martin asked.

Haley shook her head. "I don't think he was

killed at the meatpacking plant, but that's up to the police to determine." Her eyes landed on the bowl of Mr. Turner's personal items. In it was a small, folded note. She picked it up. "What's this?"

Dr. Martin shrugged. "It was in his front, right pants pocket."

Haley opened it up and read a name. "Who is Ronald Arnell?"

"I wouldn't know," Dr. Martin said.

I'll ask Samantha later if she knows the name, Haley thought.

Dr. Martin held out the scalpel. "Will you, or should I?"

"Go ahead," Haley said.

CHAPTER SIXTEEN

Samantha put down the book she was reading when she heard the lock on the door unlatch, and stepped through the double doors of the living room into the entrance. "You look tired," she said as Haley closed the door behind her.

"It's been quite a day," Haley said. She was bare-handed and without a hat, both decisions indicative of her friend's belief that comfort and convenience were more important than social propriety. Samantha wished she could be so bold. She rarely left the apartment without lipstick on, much less without the expected hat and gloves—even in summer.

"I'll heat the chicken and dumplings while you

freshen up," Samantha said, adding, "You look like you could use a drink."

After Haley had ingested her meal, they moved to the living room where Haley filled two crystal glasses with a finger of Canadian whiskey in each. The bottle was hidden out of view in a cabinet in the bookshelf.

Samantha accepted her glass and took a seat in the living room. It had a comfortable, almost masculine quality about it with its high ceilings and dark wood trim. The wallpaper lent a touch of femininity, brightening the top half of the walls. Greenery in the form of potted plants, a hanging Boston fern, and a tall Areca palm embellished the room. Plush maroon furniture faced an empty stone fireplace and a large polished wood radio. Mr. Midnight was curled up in a black, furry ball on one of the chairs, determined to ignore them.

"How much longer do you think prohibition is going to last?" Samantha asked.

Haley lounged on the couch. "Not much longer. My guess is it'll start disappearing after the next election. Most people agree it was a failed experiment."

Samantha agreed. "Definitely made the job of the police more difficult. Organized crime has never been so robust. The papers report on some of these elements every day. Al Capone is mentioned so much, I feel like I know him personally."

"A common-sense law which taxed alcohol would boost the economy."

"Lord knows the country could use that." Samantha kicked off her shoes and tucked her feet underneath herself. "So, how was your day?"

Haley sighed. "Why don't you start."

"All right. I'm no closer to finding out if Benjamin Oakes is missing or not. Wally—Doug Wallenburg—isn't the only one moving in on my story. Now Johnny is too. Not only that, Wally asked me out, sort of a working date, in front of Johnny, and Johnny got into this possessive stance, you know? Even though he's walking out with a girl, Betty Melrose."

"I thought you didn't like Mr. Wallenburg."

"It's not that I don't like him. I don't know him enough to trust him."

"And you do now?" Haley asked after a sip.

"Maybe I misjudged him. Anyway, he's investigating whether I like it or not, and I want to know what he knows. So, what took you to the meat plant?"

"Mrs. Berrymaple."

Samantha couldn't hide her surprise. "Mrs. Berrymaple? How is she involved?"

"Did you know that her husband once worked for the Oakes family at the meat plant?"

Samantha shook her head. "Mrs. Berrymaple rarely talks about her husband, except in glowing terms during moments of remembrance."

"Mr. Berrymaple was employed as a night watchman. Benjamin Oakes accused him of stealing from petty cash."

"Oh no."

"Yes, and as you can imagine, this was very distressing for Mr. and Mrs. Berrymaple. Not only was it damaging to their reputation, but it also exacerbated Mr. Berrymaple's heart condition."

"Was he fired?"

"No. Albert Oakes intervened. Unfortunately, Mr. Berrymaple died from a heart attack during this time while on the job."

"And Mrs. Berrymaple blames Ben Oakes." Understanding dawned. "Giving her motive of sorts."

"Detective Brock questioned her today," Haley said. "He was considerate enough to ask me to join him. Poor woman was rather shaken up."

Samantha felt a little shaken herself. Was the

woman she entrusted to care for her daughter capable of murder? "You don't think . . ."

"I can't imagine."

"So, what does this have to do with the meat-packing plant?"

"Mr. Berrymaple's nephew Nick also works at the plant."

"I don't understand. Does Detective Brock think Mrs. Berrymaple and the nephew were in it together?"

Haley sipped her drink. "It's a coincidence that needs investigating."

Samantha blew a raspberry. "A lot of people have access to the meat plant. It employs hundreds of men."

"Still, a lead is a lead. That's how we ended up at the plant."

Samantha's stomach clenched. "And found Mr. Turner's body. Mrs. B.'s Historical Society chum. Goldangit." She stretched out her legs. "Haley, how can I continue to let her stay with Talia? And without her, I'll have to find someone else, and I trust everyone I don't know less than I trust Mrs. B., a possible murderer."

"She's not a murderer," Haley said. "And even if

she were, she's not crazy. She loves Talia and would never harm her."

"Why do you believe she's innocent of this crime?"

"Mrs. Berrymaple had nothing against Mr. Turner. Not only that, Mrs. Berrymaple was watching Talia after school during that time, wasn't she? She was with us."

"She *was*. Mrs. B. has an alibi." The sense of relief Samantha felt was deep. "I'll look in on her tomorrow morning."

The address for Mrs. Turner's residence was included in the paperwork with Mr. Turner's body. Haley was certain that the police had already been there, firstly to inform her about her husband's death and secondly to ask questions—which was often difficult to do on the heels of bad news.

The morning was cooler than it'd been for a while, and Haley wished she'd brought her knit sweater along. Never mind. It would warm up soon enough. She approached the Turner home to offer the new widow her sympathies and hoped the lady would be ready to talk. Haley was particularly interested in what Mrs. Turner knew about the work her husband and Mrs. Berrymaple did together at the historical society.

The curtains were drawn, even though it was no longer what someone would consider early in the morning, which meant Mrs. Turner wasn't home. Maybe she'd spent the night with friends or family elsewhere. Or maybe she was grieving alone in the darkness of her kitchen.

Haley knocked. Waited. Knocked again. She was about to turn to leave when the door handle creaked, the door cracked open, and a bloodshot eye peered out at her.

"Mrs. Turner?"

"Yes."

"I'm Dr. Higgins, chief medical examiner for the City of Boston. Your husband worked with my housekeeper at the historical society, and I also had the privilege of meeting him once. I'd like to offer my deepest sympathies. Would you mind if I came in?"

Mrs. Turner hesitated, then opened the door all the way. She looked to be in her fifties, her graying hair pulled back sharply from a face etched with pain. "Forgive the mess," she said as she led the way into a small living room, opening the curtains. "I've not been myself since I heard about dear William."

"I'm so very sorry for your loss." Haley took a seat in the nearest chair.

"Would you like a cup of coffee?" Mrs. Turner asked. "The pot is on."

"That would be nice," Haley said. A cup of coffee meant Mrs. Turner expected a visit of a certain length. It would give her time to ask her questions tactfully.

The living room was filled with dated furniture and a life of collecting memories with small photographs, ceramic knickknacks, and crocheted doilies.

Haley heard coffee cups rattling on a tray and turned to see Mrs. Turner approaching. Haley jumped to retrieve the tray from the trembling woman. "Let me help you," she said, taking the tray and setting it down on the coffee table.

"I didn't know if you wanted cream and sugar," Mrs. Turner said, sitting opposite Haley. "Help yourself."

Haley took the coffee black, but Mrs. Turner poured a generous dollop of cream and two teaspoons of sugar into hers.

After a careful sip, Mrs. Turner said, "You say you knew my William?"

"I only met him once, but I could tell he was a

very nice man. A gentleman. And a curious and socially concerned person."

"Yes," Mrs. Turner said, her eyes tearing. "He was all of that. I still can't believe he's gone." She pierced Haley with her watery eyes. "The police say he was murdered. Shot." She shook her head. "It makes no sense. Everyone loved William."

In Haley's experience, she found that not everyone was loved by everyone. "Are you sure there wasn't someone your husband was at odds with?"

"If there was, I didn't know about it."

"How long had your husband volunteered at the historical society?"

"Five years. Since he retired."

"And you weren't interested in volunteering yourself?"

"Not there. I volunteer at the hospital. William and I don't . . . didn't . . . share every interest." After a long breath, she resettled her features and offered a small smile. "You said Mrs. Berrymaple is your housekeeper?"

"That's correct."

"She seemed very nice. Very eager to preserve old buildings."

Haley began carefully, "Did Mr. Turner have any

interactions or involvement with the Oakes family, the one by the docks?"

Mrs. Turner frowned. "The police asked me that as well. What is this about?"

"Probably nothing, Mrs. Turner. We're trying to rule out a connection with another murder."

"Why are you involved in the investigation? I'd think this would be the job of the police."

"I often work side by side with the police. My expertise in forensic science is helpful to them."

Mrs. Turner inclined her head. "You're an interesting woman, Dr. Higgins. Not many in this world are as manly as you."

Haley took the comment as a compliment. She smiled. "Give it time."

"Yes, well, to answer your question. William did, in fact, have an encounter with one of the Oakes brothers. About four years ago, Benjamin Oakes promised to support the society financially. Every society incurs expenses; in this case, the society wanted to purchase a building scheduled for demolition. But then Mr. Oakes broke his promise, and the building was lost to the wrecking ball."

This account supported what Detective Brock had shared with Haley, though the details of the lost building were new to her. The situation gave a motive for Mr. Turner to kill Ben Oakes, although a weak one. Would he kill someone over a building? If the bones in the morgue turned out to belong to Ben, it didn't answer why someone would then murder Mr. Turner.

Haley's remaining half cup of coffee had grown tepid. She placed it back on the tray. "Since this is a murder investigation, it may be a while before the police allow me to release the body. I'm sorry, but this will affect your funeral plans."

"I understand," Mrs. Turner said weakly. Despite the caffeine boost, the woman's complexion remained pale.

"Is there someone who can come and stay with you?" Haley asked.

"My sister is coming from New Jersey," Mrs. Turner replied. "She will be here this afternoon." Her eyes darted about the room. "I should clean up and get her bed ready."

Haley took this as her cue to leave. "Allow me to take the tray back to the kitchen."

Once the tray was delivered to the counter space by the kitchen sink, Haley said her goodbyes then headed back to the morgue. Samantha had promised to see what she could find out about Ronald Arnell. Maybe there would be a message waiting.

CHAPTER EIGHTEEN

After dropping Talia off at school, Samantha returned to the Grove Street apartment and hurried to the fourth floor. Not because she'd forgotten anything, but because she wanted to call on Mrs. Berrymaple.

Samantha's heart pinched with concern as her gaze settled on the housekeeper. "Mrs. Berrymaple?" she said as Mrs. Berrymaple opened the door. Her eyes were dull, the usual sparkle gone, and her perpetual smile lines were downward in an uncharacteristic frown.

"Oh, hello, Mrs. Rosenbaum."

"I hope you don't mind my dropping in, but I heard the news about Mr. Turner, and I'm worried about you."

"You're very kind, Mrs. Rosenbaum. I was just about to make a pot of tea. Come in."

Samantha followed Mrs. Berrymaple into the kitchen and sat at the round kitchen table as Mrs. Berrymaple served the tea. After stirring in a bit of sugar, she caught Mrs. Berrymaple's eye and said, "I'm very sorry to hear about your friend Mr. Turner. It must be very distressing."

Mrs. Berrymaple's expression crumpled. Fishing a handkerchief from her apron pocket, she dabbed at her eyes. "It is. He was a very nice man . . . and I feel awful for Mrs. Turner. I couldn't believe it when she called me. I know what it's like to lose a husband without warning. She has a tough row to hoe ahead of her."

Samantha also had some experience in this department, though she'd be lying if she said she'd shed a tear for her no-good husband. *May he rest in peace.* "Hopefully, she will have friends come around her."

"I hope so. I'll go when the time is right. It's just . . ."

"Yes?"

Mrs. Berrymaple worked the handkerchief in her hand. "The police were here yesterday morning with more questions. About Edward and Nick . . . and would you believe, my old trunk! Oh, poor Mr. Turner!"

This time, Mrs. Berrymaple couldn't contain her sobbing. Samantha rushed to her side and placed an arm around the woman's soft shoulders. "There, there. I'm sure they're just doing their job. No one in their right mind could think you capable of such a terrible crime." Samantha bit her lip. Hadn't she, even for the briefest moment, considered such a thing?

Mrs. Berrymaple patted Samantha's hand. "I'm sure you're right. I'll be fine."

Samantha returned to her seat and sipped her tea. "Do you know how your trunk ended up at the meatpacking plant?"

Mrs. Berrymaple's lips quivered as she shook her head. "None at all. I'd done a bit of spring cleaning, put old bits and pieces of things I don't use anymore into the trunk—I have no plans to travel anymore at my age—and had it picked up to take to the church flea market."

"Who picked it up for you?"

"Cole's Pickup and Delivery."

"Cole's?" Samantha wondered if this company had a connection with the groundskeeper at King's Chapel. "Are you sure about the name?"

"Yes. I still have the receipt somewhere." Mrs. Berrymaple's veiny hands went to her throat. "It's all just so dreadful. Oh, Mrs. Rosenbaum, do you think I need to get a lawyer?"

"I don't think it's as bad for you as all that." At least, Samantha hoped not. "Tell me, were you and Mr. Turner working on anything interesting recently?"

Samantha thought there had to be a reason someone wanted the man dead. And his death might have had nothing to do with the bones in the crypt.

"Mr. Turner came upon a very old letter not long ago." Mrs. Berrymaple's mouth formed a firm line. Then she said, "He'd been very excited to find it, simply due to its historical value. But . . ."

"But?"

"Well, he told me it had been penned by General Oakes' wife, Mary."

Again, the Oakes family, Samantha thought. The *coincidences* were piling up! "What did the letter say?" she asked.

"Apparently, it was a confession of sorts, a letter written to her aunt. Mrs. Oakes hinted at having had an affair during the Revolutionary War with a Loyalist soldier."

Samantha grimaced. "That would've been considered treason."

Mrs. Berrymaple agreed with a slight nod. "Which was why the letter had been so carefully hidden."

"Did she name the soldier?"

"No. In fact, the letter was carefully worded. It could be argued that her interest in the soldier was never romantic."

"Thank you for seeing me, Mrs. Berrymaple," Samantha said as she put on her hat and gloves. "I do hope you'll feel better soon. Talia was asking for you at breakfast this morning."

"I do feel better. If you like, I can pick Talia up from school."

"That would be terrific." Samantha smiled and waved at the housekeeper as she left, then hurried down the four flights of stairs to wave down a cab.

CHAPTER NINETEEN

In her line of work, Haley often met with bereaved people—husbands, wives, mothers, fathers, sons, and daughters—but it never got easier. Loss was difficult and handled in as many ways as there were people. Some became more determined to live, while others gave up on living altogether. Some found their hearts softening, their ability to embrace love stronger than ever, while others curled into themselves, blanketed in bitterness and self-pity as if the cruel world had singled them out.

Haley wondered if Mrs. Turner might turn out to be the latter. She hadn't expected much else, or at least she'd hoped for nothing else, especially anything that could've implicated Mrs. Berrymaple.

"Dr. Martin," she said on entering the morgue. "I'll be in my office if you need me."

She reclined in her chair, and then—in what was considered an unladylike action and the very reason she liked to do it—she put her feet up on her desk, crossing them at the ankles. She stared at her long calves covered in a protective sheath of silk stocking, gathered up her curls, and repinned them. She'd performed this simple task a million times without a mirror and didn't need one now. She bounced a shoe, a simple black pump with no buckles, straps, or embellishments, and thought wryly that they were the epitome of what some would call "sensible."

Some women would find that adjective offensive, determined to stay in tune with the swiftly changing fashions of the day. Haley respected that. Her good friend Ginger Gold was very fashion conscious, and Samantha tried to keep up with the trends. But Haley wasn't built that way. She'd never had that compulsion, and besides, what was wrong with being sensible? It certainly suited her line of work.

Her telephone rang, forcing Haley to put her feet back on the ground so she could reach to answer it.

"Boston City Morgue, Dr. Higgins speaking."

"Dr. Higgins, it's Detective Brock."

"Hello, Detective Brock. What can I do for you?"

The detective had her attention. He wouldn't have called if he didn't have something important to tell or ask her.

"I've heard from Scotland Yard."

"Scotland Yard?"

"It's in London."

"I am aware, Detective. I lived in London once upon a time, if you recall. I was just surprised."

"Yes, since Professor Albert Oakes claimed that his brother was living in London, healthy and well, I thought it prudent to try to confirm the fact. No one else in Boston has heard from or seen the man in over a year."

"Since the time of the missing persons' report."

"Correct. It just didn't sit right. I've had men going door-to-door, making phone calls all around Boston and anywhere else in the country where Benjamin Oakes may have had a connection. No one has seen neither hide nor hair of the man, and Scotland Yard just confirmed that a man by the name and description we've given doesn't exist there, either."

"Is it possible he's living under an assumed name?" Haley asked.

"I suppose so, but why? A man of Ben Oakes's stature doesn't change his identity and nationality for no reason. As the elder Oakes brother, he is the primary heir to the vast Oakes estate. It just doesn't make sense that he'd walk away from that without reason."

"It could be time to revisit Albert Oakes," Haley said. "Maybe he knows more than he initially let on."

"I agree," Detective Brock said. "But before we do that, I have another piece of news. Minister John Perkins reported a suspicious substance—like a pool of blood—along one of the paths in the cemetery, a trail that Minister Perkins likes to take himself. My officers took samples to the evidence laboratory, and the blood type matches William Turner's."

"Mr. Turner was shot on the burying grounds of King's Chapel?" Haley asked. "Why there? If the motive behind his death is connected with the bones, why would the killer shoot him near the crypt? Why purposely make that connection?"

"He either did it on purpose or without thinking it through," Detective Brock said. "He's either brilliant or a fool. It's up to us to figure out which one."

"What are you going to do now?" Haley asked. "And can I come along?"

"I'm planning to revisit the burying grounds, and yes."

"What about Albert Oakes?"

"I already have officers looking for him to bring him to the station."

Detective Brock hung up without saying good-bye, a social faux pas that Haley had come to expect. Pushing her curls behind her ears, she gathered her hat, gloves and purse, and made for the door.

onald Arnell.

The name reverberated in Samantha's mind as she walked toward the library. Haley had asked her to look into the name found on a scrap of paper in Mr. Turner's pocket. She had to hurry, though. Mr. August frowned when she failed to explain why she wasn't sitting at her desk writing the next fluff piece. And chances were, she'd find dozens of Ronald Arnells with no significance to this case, but if there *was* one, it could mean a break in the case and put her back on top of this story.

Samantha was so focused on the prospect that she wasn't paying close attention to her surroundings. As she headed into the library, she bumped into someone leaving, which startled her. She was even more surprised when she looked up at the cocky grin belonging to none other than Johnny Milwaukee. The library seemed to be a favorite place for journalists these days.

"Pardon me, Miss Hawke," Johnny said, tipping his hat. "You seem in an awful hurry."

"I am. You know how Mr. August gets if I'm away from my desk too much." She cast him a cheeky look. "Must be nice to be so *languid* about everything."

"Languid is my middle name. But seriously." He followed Samantha as she continued inside. "Are you still running after those bones?"

Samantha spun to face him. "There must be other murders or celebrity scandals you can chase down, Johnny. Why are you following me?"

"Truth?"

"Yes, truth, Johnny."

"You're the most interesting thing in my life right now."

Samantha blinked, uncertain how to take it. She *wanted* to be the most interesting thing in his life—she certainly found him to be interesting, but how could it possibly be so?

"You're being facetious."

"I'm not."

"I'm not sure what you want from me, Johnny. You have Betty."

Johnny flicked his fingers. "We're through."

Samantha failed to conceal her surprise. "Since when?"

"Since yesterday. She just isn't right for me. No sense draggin' things out."

Samantha parked a palm on her hip. "Are you doing this because I agreed to go out with Wally? Because that would be nuts."

"Sure, Wally got up my craw, and I don't think he's right for you."

"How can you say that?" Samantha demanded. *Are you?* She wanted to say, but the words stuck in her throat.

Johnny patted his stomach. "Gut feeling. But forget about him. Let me help you with this story. Two heads are better than one, and all that."

Samantha's memory flashed back to another time and the case on which she had worked with Johnny. After she'd done a background check on a subject, she'd also done one on Johnny Milwaukee. And immediately wished she hadn't. Not only was it unethical, but she'd learned something she wished she didn't know and had had to carry the burden of Johnny's secret with her ever since. He'd been married once before, and his wife had died along with his baby daughter. It explained his nonchalance with women. Dating was about temporary fun and not a long-term commitment. Samantha had Talia to think about, no matter what her heart longed for. Johnny was the one that was no good for her.

"I don't know," she said. "Besides, I don't have much to go on."

"Ronald Arnell?"

She stopped short. "How do you know about that name?"

"I have my sources."

"Johnny!" Samantha said, exasperated.

Johnny put a finger to his lips. "Shhh. This is a library."

"Tell me how."

"I see I've struck a nerve." Johnny smirked triumphantly.

"Johnny!"

Johnny ducked his chin and stared down Samantha with large, warm eyes, a move that often made her knees grow weak.

"How do you know about the name, Miss Hawke?" he asked. "That's the reason you're here, isn't it? I can tell by the fury on your face."

"If I am, and you were, then you already know

the information I'm looking for . . . I mean, since you were on your way out. Why don't you just tell me what you found?"

Johnny grinned that insidious, impudent, adorable grin. "And deprive you of the fun? Until later, Miss Hawke."

With tight fists, Samantha let out a low growl. A library patron scowled her way. "Quiet, Miss!"

CHAPTER TWENTY-ONE

At King's Chapel Burying Ground, Haley met Detective Brock, who'd brought along a uniformed officer. They searched for the groundskeeper, Mr. Manfred Cole, and found him trimming trees in the cemetery.

Detective Brock called out, "Mr. Cole?"

Mr. Cole turned, frowned, then forced a smile. "Hello, again."

They approached the groundskeeper, whose brow was damp with perspiration. He used a handkerchief to pat his forehead dry. "Darn humidity," he mumbled. "Now, how can I help?"

"We're looking into the death of Mr. William Turner," Detective Brock said.

"Poor soul," Mr. Cole said with a slow nod.

"Would you mind taking us to where the blood was found?" Haley asked.

Mr. Cole shrugged. "It's dried up in this heat. Not sure what's left to see."

"All the same," Detective Brock said.

After leading them to the scene, Mr. Cole said with a note of smugness, "This is the spot. Not much to see."

It did appear to be a slightly darker spot of dirt. The blood samples had already been taken, so that wasn't the purpose of this exercise. What was of interest was the proximity to the entrance of the crypt. Why had Mr. Turner come? To meet someone? To gain access to the crypt again? Was there something inside it of importance?

"Mr. Cole," Detective Brock said, stepping closer to the groundskeeper. "I have to ask you, as a matter of form—where were you two days ago, during the afternoon and onward?"

"Why?" Mr. Cole seemed stunned by the question. "Surely you can't think I had anything to do with this."

"Just a matter of form," Detective Brock repeated.

"Well, then, let me see." Mr. Cole scratched his chin. His long finger was crooked, and his nails needed cleaning. "Yes, I remember; I was listening to baseball on the radio. With my son, Manfred Junior."

"Red Sox and the Tigers?" Detective Brock said with interest.

"Yeah, that's the one."

The officer scribbled down notes, eliciting a frown from Mr. Cole.

"Does the name Ronald Arnell mean anything to you?" Haley asked.

Mr. Cole pinched his lips as he shook his head. "Don't think so. Is he a parishioner?"

Haley answered by asking another question. "Was Ben Oakes a parishioner?"

"Oh, yes. The Oakes family line goes back to the pilgrims and had ties to England like many Revolutionists had. For many years, the Oakes family had a box at the front of the church. Mr. Albert Oakes only released it to be used by others last spring."

Haley glanced at Detective Brock. That would be around the time Ben Oakes was first reported missing.

"Did either Benjamin or Albert Oakes ask to have access to the crypt around that time?" Detective Brock asked.

"As a matter of fact, before Mr. Benjamin left for England, I did take him inside the crypt."

"What was it that he hoped to see or learn?" Haley asked. "Did he say?"

"That part was rather odd, Dr. Higgins," Mr. Cole said. "He wanted to look *inside* the coffin of Mrs. Mary Oakes. He wanted me to break into the vault—even offered me money to do it, even though it was against the rules. I could've lost my job and gone to prison."

Haley had to give the man credit. Ben Oakes had been financially able to offer Mr. Cole a life-changing amount of money.

The question was: what had Ben Oakes hoped to find in his great-great grandmother's coffin? And had his search for whatever it was led to his disappearance and probable death?

"Mr. Cole," Haley started. "Didn't you say you own a truck that moves furniture or large objects around the city?"

"Oh, no, that's not me, that's my son, Manfred Junior."

Haley parked her DeSoto across the street from the warehouse area where Manfred Cole, Jr., ran his business. Detective Brock and his officer came from the other direction and parked in the nearest empty spot.

As luck would have it, a man Haley recognized

as the younger Mr. Cole stepped out of the warehouse and, with determined steps, headed to the company truck. The cab had a flat roof and window surfaces, while the body had curving lines with the standard bug-eye lamps offset from the hood. The emerald-green paint exterior was dull and dented from use, and a white-rimmed spare tire hung over the wheel well in front of the passenger door. This model had wooden slats along the side of the truck bed, making the storage area deeper.

Haley and Detective Brock left their vehicles to follow him. The detective held on to his hat as he broke into a trot. "Mr. Cole?"

The man turned. "Yeah. That's me. Whatcha want?"

Haley and the detective caught up with Manfred Junior. Unlike Senior Manfred, who'd become lean and rather frail-looking in his old age, young Manfred was a strapping, muscular version. Haley imagined days of carrying heavy furniture had helped to build his physical strength. He also lacked his father's gentle manner, and his thick brow buckled with suspicion.

Detective Brock made quick introductions. "Might we have a few moments of your time?"

"Unless you need me to move something for you . . . I'm busy."

"I think you moved a large travel trunk recently for my neighbor," Haley said. "Filled with miscellaneous household items to go to the church jumble sale?"

"Yeah, so? I move a lot of things, lady."

Haley wondered why the man was being deliberately belligerent. Detective Brock had clearly introduced her as Dr. Higgins. The demeaning use of the word "lady" was uncalled for.

"Mr. Cole," Detective Brock said sharply. "I'm investigating a murder—possibly two. You can cooperate briefly and get on with your day, or I can take you into the station to be questioned there."

Manfred Jr. folded his arms over a broad chest, his biceps bulging from under his short-sleeved shirt. The physical stance was meant to be intimidating, but Detective Brock had the weight of the law on his side.

"Git on with it then," Manfred Jr. grumbled.

"Did you pick up a travel trunk from Mrs. Edna Berrymaple and deliver it to King's Chapel on her behalf?"

"I might've."

Haley scowled. When jobs were so scarce, how was it that a creep like Manfred Cole Jr. was gainfully employed? "What day was this delivery?" she asked.

"I dunno, ma'am. I don't got my schedule memorized."

"Can you look it up?" Detective Brock said, keeping cool as a cucumber. "You must keep records."

Manfred Jr. huffed, opened his truck cab, and removed a notebook. "I write down all my appointments here." He flipped back several pages, then stabbed an entry with his finger. "Last Wednesday, eleven a.m."

"Did you happen to have a look inside the trunk?" Detective Brock asked.

"No. Not my business." He shrugged. "The old lady hardly seemed the sort to be movin' stuff on the black market."

"Mr. Cole," Haley started, "do you happen to know a Mr. Benjamin Oakes?"

Another huff. "Sure. Stuffed shirt. Doesn't run in my circles, if you know what I mean."

"But you knew him?" Haley pressed. "Did you ever meet in person?"

"Hey." Manfred Cole Junior wrinkled his short nose. "What is this all about, anyway?" He pointed to a clunky watch on his wrist. "I got a pickup to make."

"Just answer the question," Detective Brock said.

"Okay. Fine. Yeah, we met. The scum was harassing my old man. I roughed him up."

"Roughed him up?" Haley said. "Please be more specific."

"I dunno. He wanted my old man to chip out the brick wall of the vault, and when he refused, Ben Oakes threatened him. So, I threatened him back."

"How?" Detective Brock said. "How did you threaten him?"

"I might've pushed him up against a wall, nothing serious. Might've put my face in his and told him to lay off my old man or he'd be sorry. It was a bluff. I wasn't really gonna do anything. I just wanted him to back off, ya know?"

"Did you cause him any physical harm?" Haley asked.

"Look, the guy was a toothless tiger. Thought he was a big shot. He threw a punch, which I stopped with one fist, and he started crying like his dad just gave him the belt. Went on about his finger hurting."

"The little finger of his right hand?"

"Maybe. I don't know. He was holding his hurt hand with the other one. I might've broke something. Is that his beef? I don't know why he'd send you to hound me after all this time. That was more than a year ago."

"You haven't seen Mr. Benjamin Oakes since that encounter?" Detective Brock asked.

"Nope. Now, can I go?"

Detective Brock nodded slowly. "Thank you for your time, Mr. Cole."

"Mr. Cole," Haley said, turning back to face the man. "Did you listen to that last Red Sox game?"

Mr. Cole wrinkled his nose. "Yeah. This is Boston. Who wouldn't?"

"Did you listen to it with your dad?"

"Yeah, so?"

Haley nodded. "Have a good day, Mr. Cole."

As Detective Brock walked Haley back to her car, he asked, "Does that make sense? Our skeleton has a missing little finger, and Mr. Cole admits to having broken it. Are the two connected?"

"It could be that Mr. Oakes died before healing could begin on the bone, and it fell out somewhere. It's possible if it was a clean break on a knuckle."

"Ouch."

"Or it could be that Mr. Oakes lost a finger earlier in his life, and the broken bone if one had actually fractured, had healed before his death." Haley unlocked the car door and opened it. "I'll head back to the morgue and have another look."

CHAPTER TWENTY-TWO

Samantha left the library feeling torn. She should return to the pen before Mr. August assumed she was slacking, and fired her. On the other hand, she had news that Haley would find interesting.

On the *other*, other hand, she could relay her news over the telephone on her desk. But the guys there were big snoops and would listen to her conversation. They did this often, even though they weren't good at pretending. Samantha could tell when they were eavesdropping.

No, she'd stop in at the morgue for a short time, then get back to the pen and hammer out the fluff piece Mr. August was waiting for. As long as she had it on his desk by three o'clock, he would be appeased.

It was a quick taxi ride to the hospital. Inside, Samantha held the rail as she carefully maneuvered down the steps in her new three-inch heels. She justified new purchases by telling herself she needed to look professional for work but had to admit the extra inch on a pointier heel wasn't conducive to good reporting. She just hoped she wouldn't find herself in a position where she needed to run.

The heavy door of the morgue was closed as expected. She knocked, then cracked it open. "Dr. Higgins?"

Haley's voice came back. "Oh, come in, Samantha."

Samantha stepped inside the morgue, giving her nose a moment to adjust to the smells. Although the smell indicated plenty of bleach and scented cleaners were in use, the dank scent of death still permeated through.

Her gaze stayed on Haley who, using a magnifying glass, was intently staring at the bones of the crypt skeleton, now laid out on a secondary table, one not designed for surgical procedures like a postmortem.

"What's up?" Samantha said.

Haley placed the magnifying glass on a nearby shelf. "Manfred Cole's son, Manfred Junior. admitted to accosting Ben Oakes."

"Whatever for?"

"For pressuring Mr. Cole Senior into opening Mrs. Mary Oakes's coffin. Apparently, Mr. Oakes uttered threats when Mr. Cole Senior refused."

"What were you looking for?" Samantha asked.

"Mr. Cole Junior says Mr. Ben Oakes threw a punch, which Mr. Cole Junior stopped with his oversized fist. He alluded to the possibility that he could've broken something."

"Like a finger?"

Haley nodded. "I considered the possibility, but it's more likely that Mr. Oakes had lost his finger before this crushing event."

"Do we know for sure that these bones belong to Benjamin Oakes?"

"Not unequivocally," Haley said. "But the bones of the right hand of this man did suffer stress not long before he died. Two bones have slight hairline fractures."

Haley washed her hands in the porcelain sink then invited Samantha into her office. "Let's get off our feet."

Samantha was grateful for the offer as her new shoes pinched her toes.

"Would you like tea or coffee?" Haley asked. "I can ask Dr. Martin to brew a pot."

Samantha would've loved to accept either tea or coffee but shook her head. "I'm pushed for time. Mr. August will have my head if I don't get back to the pen soon."

Haley sat behind her desk as Samantha took a facing chair.

"Then you must have something important to tell me," Haley said.

"I don't know if it's important or simply interesting, but I didn't want to give the guys in the pen a chance to overhear."

"I'm intrigued," Haley said. "What's it about?"

"Ronald Arnell. You asked me to see what I could find on him."

"Yes. The scribbled name on the scrap of paper in Mr. Turner's pocket."

"Surprisingly, there are very few Arnells living in Boston, and none with Ronald as a first name. But I did find a record of an American soldier who fought in the Revolutionary War."

"I'd think this is insignificant," Haley said, "if it weren't for the fact that the bones were placed in front of a coffin belonging to a general in that same war."

"Exactly," Samantha said eagerly. "So, I kept digging. He served in the Third Massachusetts Regiment."

"Not far from the Oakes estate. It's possible he was acquainted with the Oakeses."

"Not possible, probable," Samantha said. "Sergeant Arnell was under General Oakes' command. During the heat of battle, soldiers sometimes took leave on the property. A barn was outfitted for such a purpose."

Haley pursed her lips. "The plot thickens."

"And here's where it gets interesting. Sergeant Arnell defected to the Loyalist side and gave away secrets that led to an attack on American forces."

Haley gasped. "Not unlike Benedict Arnold. You're right, Sam. This *is* interesting. But how does it tie in to the present-day Oakes family?"

"Oh, I know," Samantha said. "Mrs. Berrymaple said that Mr. Turner had found a letter written by Mrs. Mary Oakes where she appeared to be admitting to an affair." A feeling of excitement twirled in her stomach, as it always did when she felt like a story was about to break. "Do you think—?"

Haley held up a palm. "We mustn't jump to

conclusions just yet. Everything is circumstantial. One thing *seems* connected to another, but we don't have real proof."

Samantha slumped, feeling a touch deflated. Haley was right. An excellent investigative reporter didn't speculate. She investigated. "What should we do now?"

"We need to find Albert Oakes," Haley said. "I sense he might have the puzzle pieces we're looking for."

Samantha stood. "Let me know when we can work that out. But for now, I have to run. I need to tap out a thousand words on how to make elderflower cordial."

CHAPTER TWENTY-THREE

*B*uses and trams moved regularly throughout all the districts in Boston, and many people rode public transit into Cambridge, where Harvard University was located. A telephone call to the Oakes mansion confirmed Professor Albert Oakes had gone to the university to catch up on grading papers. Samantha and Haley wanted to get there quickly, and going by car meant they would reach their destination in under an hour, providing the roads remained clear of stalled vehicles or broken-down carriages. Besides, it was a nice drive on a warm day, rumbling over Longfellow Bridge with captivating views of the Charles River and then down the long street of Broadway.

Haley parked her DeSoto in one of the campus's

parking lots. Samantha stared at the greenery of the surrounding space and the impressive brick buildings dotted about the property with a look of awe. "I've never set foot here before," she confessed.

"I suppose you've never had a reason before now."

"It's little more than a gentlemen's club for the rich," Samantha said with disdain, her eyes following small groups of students moving from building to building, all males.

Haley didn't disagree. "Female students were relegated to Radcliffe College, considered a 'Harvard Annex' for women, which is why I attended Boston University. It's not segregated by gender."

"Very progressive," Samantha said. "Do you know where we're going?"

Haley pointed. "There's the science building. I imagine Professor Oakes has an office in there."

The campus was a mix of newer and historical buildings dotted about a massive park-like setting. One of the newer ones was the Mallinckrodt Chemical Laboratory, a robust red-brick building with a facade of Grecian-style columns at the entrance.

Inside, a map of the building was fixed to the wall with a corresponding menu listing the professors' classes and laboratories. Albert Oakes was listed.

Samantha and Haley followed the directions to his office.

Haley tapped on the door, which was ajar. "Professor Oakes?"

The sound of a man clearing his throat was followed by, "Yes, come in."

The office had full bookshelves, student papers piled on the oak desk, and a scattering of school-themed photos. Professor Oakes' credentials were framed and hanging on the wall behind him.

Albert Oakes stared back at Samantha and Haley with disdain. "Again? I thought I answered your questions yesterday."

"We have a few more," Samantha said, claiming a chair. "If you don't mind."

Albert clasped his hands and propped them on his slight belly. "I suspect it won't matter if I do mind."

Samantha glanced at Haley, who remained on her feet, slowly walking about the room, staring at items on the many shelves and the paintings hanging on the wall.

Albert's seemingly uneasy gaze followed her.

"Still no word from your brother?" Samantha asked.

Albert narrowed his eyes. "Not since yesterday, Miss Hawke."

"Did Benjamin suffer from any bone diseases?" Haley asked.

"I'm not sure what that has to do with anything," the man blustered, "but yes, he had a weakening spine. Pott's disease. Suffered from severe back pain." He smirked, "His ailment was well known by anyone who knew him."

Haley turned to catch his eye. "What do you know about Sergeant Arnell, Professor Oakes?"

Albert pulled himself up stiffly. "Why should I know anything?"

"Well, I thought since your brother was a professor of history, that you and he may have discussed certain things of note," Haley answered. "Things like the Revolutionary War, especially the interesting parts concerning treason."

"Oh, yes, *that* Sergeant Arnell. He was an American soldier who defected to the Loyalists. It wasn't that uncommon, you know. Many American soldiers became disgruntled and disillusioned during that time. There were similar events during the Great War as well."

"Did you know that this particular Sergeant Arnell served under your great-great grandfather?"

Samantha asked. "It's reported that he spent some leave time on your property."

A wave of crimson crept up Albert's neck into his cheeks. He bit out, "What exactly do you ladies want from me? I'm not in the mood for a trip down memory lane."

"I've learned that the general's wife had an affair," Samantha said. "Probably with an American soldier who lived on your estate for some time, possibly with Sergeant Arnell."

Albert shot to his feet. "That's enough. I'll not have you stir up slander just so you can sell a few newspapers, Miss Hawke."

Albert stormed out of the office. Haley shared a look of interest with Samantha then turned to gather up her purse. Her eyes landed on an old framed photograph propped up on the sheltered shelving. She pulled it out from behind a book lying flat on its cover. It appeared to be a family photo, a more youthful Albert and Benjamin flanking their parents. Haley quickly retrieved the magnifying glass she kept in her purse and poised it over the image of Benjamin Oakes.

"What do you see?" Samantha asked her.

"It's what I don't see," Haley said, handing the glass to Samantha.

"Aha," Samantha said. Young Benjamin was missing the tip of his right baby finger.

THE DRIVE back into Boston seemed interminable to Haley, the traffic heavy and slow. She was tempted more than once to reach out her window and squeeze her brass horn's rubber ball.

"It's getting so bad," Samantha said with shared exasperation, "we might as well go back to horse and buggy."

"Mornings and afternoons are the worst," Haley agreed. "More people driving to get to work."

"We know the bones belong to Benjamin Oakes," Samantha said.

"With ninety-eight percent certainty."

"What would make it one hundred percent?"

"A confession."

"I want to write the story."

Haley geared down, having approached the bumper of the car in front of her. "You don't have the whole thing."

"I'll write what we do know. If I don't do it, Johnny or Wally will."

Haley understood Samantha's urgency. "I'll drop you off at the paper before I go to the precinct."

It seemed to take Haley forever to get to the police station, and even then, she had no reassurance that Detective Brock would be there. If only there were such a thing as a car telephone!

As luck would have it, Detective Brock was at his desk when Haley knocked on his office door. He glanced up, his smile deepening then falling as concern took over his expression.

"Dr. Higgins, is everything all right?"

"I'm almost certain that the bones found in the crypt belong to Benjamin Oakes."

"Please," the detective said, waving to an empty chair. "Have a seat."

Haley sat, taking a moment to catch her breath. "Albert Oakes is lying."

"What have you learned?"

"Samantha and I went to visit him at Harvard—"

"I bet the traffic was horrendous."

Haley shot him a look. "It was. Especially over the bridge."

"I rarely leave Boston if I can help it."

"Yes, well, Sam and I endured the headaches to get there. I asked Albert Oakes if he or Benjamin ever suffered from a bone disease, and he answered, perhaps without regard to possible implications, but most likely because anyone who knew Ben Oakes was aware of his affliction."

"Don't tell me. Benjamin had Pott's disease?"

"Yes. Not only that, Albert also had an old photograph of his family on a cluttered shelf. He might've even forgotten it was there. And in it, Benjamin is clearly missing a part of his little finger. Albert lied to my face about the fact."

Detective Brock picked up the black telephone receiver from its cradle and tucked it between his ear and shoulder.

"What are you doing?" Haley asked.

"Calling a judge for a warrant."

"To where?"

"Good question. Harvard, home, or both?"

"Go for both, if you can get it, but I'd start with his home."

Detective Brock nodded. "My thoughts exactly."

CHAPTER TWENTY-FOUR

Giving the guys a cursory nod, Samantha made a beeline to her desk, placed her purse, hat, and gloves in the large bottom drawer, and inserted a piece of paper into the roller.

"What's got you tied up in knots, doll?" Johnny said casually. "I hope you're not writing about Ronald Arnell?"

Samantha snapped her gaze to Johnny's. "What are you talking about?"

"I'm just saying that ship has sailed." Johnny sauntered over and dropped the morning edition of *The Boston Daily Record* on Sam's desk, folded open to the human-interest section. Samantha had been so busy all day she'd only read the front page over breakfast.

The headline of Johnny's piece read: "American Traitor or Hero?"

Samantha felt the heat of frustration and anger bloom across her chest. Why did Johnny have to nose in on her leads? A quick read showed that he'd stuck to historical facts with nothing to tie the interest piece to the murder of William Turner. She feigned indifference. "Very nice, Johnny. Now, if you don't mind, I have work."

She was glad she hadn't started typing, and it was obvious that Johnny was looking at the blank sheet.

"I know, doll. I know. But as they say, 'All work and no play makes Jack a dull boy.' Or, in your case, Jane a dull girl."

"What's your point?" Samantha said with exasperation.

"I think you need some playtime." He grinned. "With me."

Samantha swallowed. The room got suddenly quiet. A glance showed all the men in the room had paused what they were doing to listen. Wally scowled. Samantha regretted that careless offer to go out with him.

Before Samantha could reply, Johnny continued. "How about dinner and a movie? *The Sign of Four,* the Sherlock Holmes flim is playing. Have you seen it?"

Of course, Samantha hadn't seen it. When did she have time to go to the movies? She was working or caring for her daughter. She lamely shook her head as her stomach did a quick somersault. Going on a proper date with Johnny Milwaukee had been her ongoing fantasy for months.

Johnny continued brazenly. "How about Friday?"

Wally bellowed, "Hey! Sam said she'd go out with me."

What a nightmare. Samantha had never wanted to go out with Wally in the first place, but Johnny, the cad, boldly called out the one night he knew she was busy with Wally.

Men!

"Johnny, I'm busy right now. Maybe we can talk later." She raised a brow. "When we don't have an audience?"

"Sure thing, doll." He smirked, then turned and walked away.

Samantha started writing, holding in a wry grin. Clearly, Johnny and Wally didn't know that the identity of the bones had been confirmed. As they were busy peacocking, she was on her way to another scoop.

CHAPTER TWENTY-FIVE

At the Oakes residence, Haley expected Ellsworth to answer the resounding gong, but instead, after Detective Brock rang for a second time, a tired-looking maid opened the door. Her eyes rounded in question at the small gathering on the front steps. Four uniformed officers, including Officer Bell, had accompanied them to help with the search.

Detective Brock produced the warrant.

"What is it?" the maid said, fear flashing behind her eyes.

"Is Mr. Oakes available?" Detective Brock asked.

The maid shook her head. "Come back another time." She started closing the door, but Detective

Brock stepped on the threshold, stopping her. "Miss, I'm afraid this piece of paper, signed by a judge, means you must let us in. We are here as part of an investigation into a crime."

The maid tried to protest but quickly realized her efforts would be in vain. She disappeared soon after Haley and the men filled the entranceway. Detective Brock instructed his officers to begin with the upstairs bedrooms. "You should be able to determine which one belongs to Albert Oakes."

Haley called Detective Brock to join her in the sitting room and gestured to the portraits on the walls.

"The family tree?" Detective Brock said.

Haley pointed to the one that interested her the most. "That is General John Oakes, and the woman is his wife, Mary."

"How are these two, who've been dead for so long, tied to these deaths?" Detective Brock asked.

"Hopefully, we'll find out today."

Haley pointed out the photograph of the most recent branch of the Oakes family tree. "The younger boy is Albert," Haley said. "The family resemblance is strong throughout the line. The older one is almost a cookie cutter of the younger one, though now I can see how his shoulders are hunched. Evidence of spinal tuberculosis."

Detective Brock hummed. "And the missing fingertip is clear as well. Do we know how he lost it?"

"No. Albert would know, but he insisted his brother still possessed all his phalanges."

"Curious," Detective Brock said. "The butler—"

"Ellsworth."

"He's been with the family a long time?"

Haley gave him a sideways glance. "According to Albert, yes."

"Maybe he can fill in a few blanks."

They moved into a connecting room that appeared to be a study. From the papers and books on the desk and built-in wooden shelves—everything tidy and in place—they determined it was where Albert worked from home.

Haley searched the desk drawers. A sheet of paper folded to fit neatly into an envelope rested on the top of a pile of pens, not put away with his other correspondence. Haley thought it unusual, given the orderliness of everything else in the room. Opening it, she scanned the contents.

"Detective Brock?"

The detective spun toward the voice. "Uh-huh."

"This is a letter from Benjamin Oakes, the one Albert claimed proved his brother was still alive."

Detective Brock stared down at the sheet of paper in Haley's hands. "November sixth, 1931. That would make it impossible for the bones to belong to him." He locked his eyes on Haley. "Is it possible an error was made?"

Haley shook her head. "No. The bones are Ben's." Retrieving her magnifying glass from her purse, she held it over the date. "Look. The three is an alteration. It originally read 1921."

"Why would Albert go to the trouble," Detective Brock said, "unless he believed he'd have to cover his tracks. And why would he do that unless he was guilty?"

"If Albert killed his brother, then we must assume he probably killed William Turner as well." Haley moved quietly about the office. "The question is why? What motive did he have?"

"Sex, money, revenge? These are the top three."

"There's been no indication that sex is the motive, as no women are involved in the case so far. And money doesn't seem to be a problem."

Detective Brock agreed. "I had a look into the

family finances. Nothing in arrears. The estate has enough money to care for itself—taxes, upkeep, and whatnot."

"Revenge, then?"

Officer Bell's voice followed a soft tap on the open door's frame. "Sir?"

"What did you find?"

Officer Bell held out a sheet of paper, which, unlike Benjamin's letter, was thin and yellow. Haley glanced at the sheet. "Mary Oakes?"

"Yes, ma'am."

To Detective Brock, she said, "I stand corrected. A woman does feature in this case." This letter was more direct in Mary's admission. She'd grown bold during her dying days, releasing the bitterness she held against General Oakes.

He repeatedly accused me of barrenness when it was he, *not I, who was to be blamed for that.*

Turning to Officer Bell, Haley asked, "Was this found in Albert Oakes's bedroom?"

Officer Bell shook his head. "No, ma'am. Holt found it in the servants' area. The bedroom belonging to the butler."

Haley shot Detective Brock a look. *The butler?*

"Does Ellsworth know you've been in his room?" Detective Brock asked.

"I don't think so. He wasn't on the premises then, but I believe he's returned since."

"Thank you, Bell," Detective Brock said. "Please bring Mr. Ellsworth to the station for questioning. And while you're at it, track down Professor Albert Oakes and bring him in too."

Walter Ellsworth sat upright in a wooden straight-backed chair in the interrogation room, emanating indignation like dark waves. Here was a man used to propriety and order with English sensibilities. He lived to serve the family who'd employed him for over fifty years. Haley could see the wheels turning behind the man's cold, angry eyes as if his mind was silently protesting: *Outrageous! Preposterous! How dare they?*

Normally, Haley wouldn't be part of the closed-room interrogation at the police station. Still, Detective Brock's predecessor, Detective Cluney, had praised her intelligence, insight, and positive contributions to detective work. Detective Brock had discovered these values true when working together on an earlier case.

Detective Brock entered the room hatless, his hair parted sharply on one side and smoothed over with hair oil. His abrupt and often brash ways were idiosyncrasies that were growing on Haley.

Officer Bell stood at the door should the butler have the sudden urge to bolt.

Detective Brock sat across the table from the butler. "Mr. Ellsworth, do you know why you're here?"

"I do not," Mr. Ellsworth replied tersely. "I do hope you're about to explain adequately."

"I am," Detective Brock said with a nod. He glanced at Haley seated beside him, then said, "We regret to inform you that Mr. Benjamin Oakes is dead."

Mr. Ellsworth remained emotionless. Were years of practice at being stoic on display, or was he simply not surprised because he already knew?

"I'm very sorry to hear that," he finally said.

"You don't seem surprised, Mr. Ellsworth," Haley stated.

"Mr. Ben has been gone a long time, madam. It crossed my mind he may have come to a bad end."

"Except that his brother, Albert, states that he's alive and well in England," Detective Brock added.

"That was my hope—"

"But?" Haley said.

"I hadn't received any correspondence from him."

Detective Brock braced his elbows on his knees. "And you expected to? As the butler?"

"I've been with the family for nearly half a century, sir. Their father brought me on. I acted as his valet when he married and was there at the time both sons came into the world. Once Mr. and Mrs. Oakes were gone, you could say I was all the lads had left."

"You're very devoted," Haley stated.

"Indeed, madam."

"What happens to the estate upon Albert's death?" Detective Brock asked.

"I'm not privy to that information. I assume the estate will dissolve with proceeds going to wherever Mr. Albert dictates in his will."

"And you've never seen the will," Detective Brock pushed. "You're not a beneficiary?"

"I have not seen the will, and I have no way of knowing if I am to benefit. If so, I'm assuming I'll be granted enough to carry me to the end of my days and no more. It's not uncommon for long-time employees to be provided for to a certain degree."

"Does the name Ronald Arnell mean anything to you?" Haley asked.

Mr. Ellsworth's face grew pink. "I can't think why it should."

Haley tapped a finger on the tabletop. "Did you read the article in this morning's *Boston Daily Record*?"

"It was absolute rubbish!"

"It's historically accurate," Haley said. "You appear to be taking the matter personally."

Mr. Ellsworth pinched his lips together as if forcing the rebuttal forming there to submit to silence.

Detective Brock decided this was the moment to present the letter written by Mary Oakes. "What can you tell me about this?"

Shocked, Mr. Ellsworth stared back with barely contained fury. "You were in my room?"

"We had a judge's warrant to search the entire manor, Mr. Ellsworth," Detective Brock said. "Search warrants aren't that hard to come by when a murder is suspected."

"Whose murder would that be?"

"Benjamin Oakes's, for one. William Turner's for

another. Now . . ." Detective Brock poked the old letter with his index finger. "What was this letter doing in your room, and what does it mean to you?"

"I think I'd like to ring a solicitor."

Detective Brock cocked his head. "You haven't been accused of anything. If you answer my questions, I can let you go."

"I'll take my chances with a solicitor."

A knock at the door was followed by a low-volume message being given to Officer Bell.

"What is it, Officer?" Detective Brock asked.

"It's about the other suspect, sir."

"Professor Oakes?"

Haley shot the detective a look. Normally, he'd be more discreet in front of another suspect unless he purposely intended to use this information to rile up the butler.

It worked.

"Professor Oakes had nothing to do with it," Mr. Ellsworth said. "It was me."

Detective Brock leaned in. "Are you confessing, Mr. Ellsworth?"

"I am."

"To what crime, exactly."

Mr. Ellsworth's eyes rounded as his gaze darted about the room.

He's fishing for an answer, Haley thought.

The clock on the wall ticked loudly.

"Mr. Ellsworth?" Detective Brock pressed. "What is your crime?"

"Murder. I killed Mr. Ben."

"And how, exactly, did you do that?"

Tick, tock, tick, tock.

"I stabbed him."

"And what did you do with the body?"

"I hid it in the cellar."

"For how long."

"Months."

"How many months?"

Perspiration formed on Mr. Ellsworth's brow. "I don't know. A year or so. I didn't keep track of the time. But . . ." His head jerked up. "I moved the bones to the King's Chapel crypt."

"That information was provided in the papers," Haley said. "Can you tell us something a subscriber to the local papers wouldn't know?"

Mr. Ellsworth bit his lip, then said, "I would like a solicitor."

CHAPTER TWENTY-SEVEN

Haley and Detective Brock left Mr. Ellsworth in the interrogation room with Officer Bell, who would lead the butler to a holding cell. In the small precinct kitchen, they each filled a mug from the coffee percolator. It looked overly dark and smelled strong. Haley wished sugar was more readily available, but it seemed the police station was also cutting corners. She took a tentative sip, grimacing slightly as she swallowed.

"So," she started. "The butler did it?"

"Crimes committed by domestic staff are more common than you would think," Detective Brock said. "You know, I just read a murder mystery novel —not by Christie, but one of those other crime-writing ladies—where the butler *did* do it."

Haley stared at the detective, feeling a sense of shock. Not that someone had written a crime novel where the butler was guilty, but that the detective read such books. Haley's reading consisted primarily of scientific journals and reports. Maybe she should read more fiction.

"Something seems off to me," Haley said. "Why suddenly confess like that? It's like he's afraid of what Albert Oakes will say when you interview him."

"We don't have Albert Oakes."

Haley's jaw dropped. "What?"

"That was a ruse. Butlers are notoriously loyal. I thought he might give something away in an attempt to protect Albert. I didn't imagine he'd confess to the crime."

"It's the ultimate sacrifice," Haley said. "Ellsworth didn't know enough details to convince me. However, he might convince a jury in time. Do you know if he had any connection with William Turner?"

Detective Brock shook his head. "That is unknown at this time."

"So where is Albert Oakes?"

"That is a good question, Dr. Higgins. I've got my men looking." Detective Brock smiled. "Would you like to grab something to eat while we're waiting?"

Samantha delivered her story about the crypt bones belonging to Benjamin Oakes to Mr. August. The editor pushed up his round spectacles as he pinched the sheet of paper with nicotine-stained fingers. After reading, he stared at Samantha over the rims of his spectacles.

"You sure about this?"

"The chief medical examiner has confirmed it."

"All right then." After signing off, he held the sheet out to her. "Take it down to composing."

Samantha held in the shock she felt. Usually, the editor ran his red pencil through the copy, marking it up for changes. This was the first time he'd handed it back clean with just his scribbled signature on the bottom.

"Yes, sir," she said. She left for the stairs that led to the lower level, where the tedious work of composing took place and where the darkroom was located. She nearly bumped into Johnny, who was coming up the other side.

"Ronald Arnell," he said. "He's tied up in this

Oakes case somehow, doll. I just can't seem to crack it."

For once, Samantha didn't feel like pushing Johnny out of her way. He was right. She hadn't given this particular clue enough thought. "He served under General Oakes," she said.

Johnny stepped closer. "And took leave on the estate property."

Samantha was suddenly hyper-aware of Johnny's cologne. She swallowed hard as she said, "Mrs. Oakes' letter references an illicit assignation."

Johnny leaned in. The stairwell seemed to close in on Samantha and her good senses. "It could've resulted in a child."

She jerked back, hit with a new and probable theory as to why Benjamin Oakes was killed. "I've gotta go."

Samantha took a step up before recalling the reason she was headed down in the first place. She shoved the sheet to Johnny. "Can you give this to Inky, please? I have to make a telephone call."

HALEY SAT across from Detective Brock at a sandwich shop. It wasn't a date. It was just work happening over a meal. Yet, she found herself thinking that she wouldn't mind it, maybe, if it were a date. That was if there wasn't such an intriguing case that needed solving first.

Detective Brock—*Nolan,* could she ever call him by his first name? She couldn't imagine it—wolfed down the first half of his ham and cheddar cheese sandwich, then said, "We are missing motive. What ties Benjamin Oakes to William Turner?"

Haley had been making mental lists about this very question. "The crypt at King's Chapel. Ben Oakes's ancestors are buried there. William Turner was a member of the Historical Society with keen interest in preserving the crypt."

"Maybe Turner had learned about the altercation between Ben Oakes and Cole?"

"I'd really like to know what Ben Oakes hoped to find. It was Mary Oakes's coffin he wanted opened, wasn't it?"

Detective Brock nodded. "My guess? Ben was looking for something."

"A letter written by Mary Oakes?" Haley ventured. "What else could've been buried with her that could be so incriminating so many years later?"

"That's the question. What could the matriarch have seen or done or said that would bother Ben Oakes so dearly now?"

"The family tree." Haley tapped her mouth with a napkin. "The Oakes family reputation was at risk of being irreparably damaged. Even annihilated."

"What do you mean?"

"What if Benjamin and Albert aren't from the general's line but from that of a traitor to the nation?"

Detective Brock's jaw dropped. "Are you saying that Benjamin and Albert's ancestry lead back to Mrs. Oakes and Ronald Arnell?"

"It's a theory."

"That's the kind of information a person might not want to become public."

"The kind of information someone might kill to keep quiet."

Detective Brock opened his wallet and tossed a bill on the table. "We need to find Albert Oakes."

"I agree, but I can pay for my own sandwich."

Detective Brock's lips tugged up to one side. "No time, Doctor. No time."

CHAPTER TWENTY-EIGHT

Samantha's efforts to reach Haley were in vain. She was neither at the morgue nor the apartment. She then called the Oakes residence —the call answered by the housemaid—and the office at Harvard, neither of which could produce Albert Oakes. Her mind raced. *What to do?* If she were Albert trying to flee the country, where would she go? *The ferry terminal.* It was the only way to get from the North End to the airport in East Boston. But she had no car! How would she get there quickly?

Johnny.

"Johnny!"

Everyone in the pen turned to her shrill call, but Johnny's desk was empty.

"Sam?"

Samantha turned to Wally's voice. "Do you have a car here, Wally?"

Wally shook his head. "I walk to work."

"What's goin' on?"

Samantha spun on her heel at Johnny's voice. She grabbed his hand. "I need you to drive me somewhere. I'll share the byline."

Johnny opened his desk drawer and produced a set of keys. "Let's go, then. Umm, where are we goin'?"

Samantha waited until they were outside and heading toward Johnny's red roadster. "I think Ben Oakes' killer is dodging the country."

"And you know his killer now?" He slid into the driver's seat as Samantha entered the passenger side. "How's that?"

"Call it a hunch, Johnny. But Albert is the only remaining member of the Oakes family line. He'd want to preserve the reputation of his family name, especially since he was vying for the position of president at Harvard."

"Which is why he killed his brother?"

"If his brother had damaging information about his lineage."

"Is Albert in danger of being caught?"

"I don't know. But what matters is whether he thinks he's in danger of being caught. I believe he's heading to the airport. We need to get to the ferry terminal before he catches the next boat."

"All right, doll, though I think we're digging for a needle in a haystack."

The ferry terminal was a humble wood structure, just large enough to hold a ticket seller, a sandwich stand, and to shelter waiting passengers. When the ferry arrived, a gangway connecting it to dry land was propped up.

Samantha searched the faces of the passengers, looking for Albert.

"Do you see him?" Johnny asked.

"No, but I see *him.*"

Johnny squinted. "Who?"

"The butler. Walter Ellsworth."

Haley followed Detective Brock outside and kept up with the man's long strides as he headed for the nearest police telephone. He dialed.

"Where's Albert Oakes now?" Haley shot him a look.

Detective Brock mouthed, "I had him followed." Brock hesitated. "I see," he said to the officer on the other end of the line. "Wait, what? How in the blazes did that happen? Yeah, well, there'll be time for excuses later. Send backup to the ferry terminal. I'm heading there now." He slammed down the receiver.

"What's going on?" Haley asked.

"Ellsworth slipped out of the station."

"How'd he do that? Wasn't Officer Bell watching him?"

"Bell passed on the duty to a rookie. Ellsworth can come off quite grandfatherly, and the rookie underestimated the man." He snorted his derision. "Ellsworth asked to use the facilities, and that was the last anyone saw of him." Pointing, he added, "My car is here."

The car was a police-issued Ford Model B. Haley would pick up her DeSoto later. The advantage the police car had was the siren. The squeal and light combination worked wonders in getting vehicles, pedestrians, horses, and buggies to move out of the way.

"Your men are still on his tail?" Haley asked.

"Yup. We're heading to the ferry again."

Two other police vehicles were parked near the ferry terminal entrance when Detective Brock suddenly stopped. Haley wasn't sure what they'd find inside. Hopefully, Albert was already in custody and handcuffed. They walked from the car to the terminal building, but Haley wasn't prepared for what she saw inside. The crowd had dispersed like water when hit with a drop of oil. In the center of the near-empty terminal was a woman at the mercy of an armed man.

Haley's voice came out as a whisper. "Samantha?"

"It's the damn butler," Detective Brock muttered. He held up his palms and said smoothly. "Mr. Ellsworth. Let the woman go."

"Miss Hawke was going to reveal all the family secrets," the butler said with eerie calm. "I can't let that happen."

"It's too late," Detective Brock said. "If she doesn't do it, someone else will."

Haley watched with surprise as Johnny Milwaukee approached from behind. "The feathers are out of the bag, mister."

As the butler twisted to the sound of Johnny's voice, he loosened his grip on Samantha. Just as Johnny bodychecked the man, she ducked and spun out of the butler's hold. The gun slid across the floor, where Albert Oakes slid to meet it from out of nowhere. Johnny had Ellsworth's arm pushed up his spine, with the older man calling out in pain. Detective Brock snapped on the cuffs. "You're under arrest for the murders of—"

His sentence dropped when he spotted Albert—gun in hand and pointed at Haley.

"Mr. Oakes." Haley slowly raised her arms. "There's no need to panic. Put the gun down."

"Why? You and your nosy friend have ruined everything." His lower lip quivered. "Everything my family built our name on is gone."

Haley was at a loss for words. What he said was true; nothing she could say would comfort him. The best she could do was elicit a confession and hope she didn't die doing it.

"Did you kill your brother, Mr. Oakes?"

He sighed; the hand holding the gun trembled. "I had no choice. He was going to tell the world the truth about our heritage."

"That you and he came from the line of Ronald Arnell and not from General Oakes?"

"Yes! *That*! So damning!"

"Albert!" The bellow came from the characteristically quiet butler. "Shut up!"

Haley started to lower her arms, but Albert trained his gun back on her. "Is that why you killed William Turner?" Haley asked.

Albert blinked. "No. I didn't kill him." He flicked his gun toward Ellsworth. "He did that."

"Will you shut your bloody mouth, Albert," Ellsworth spat. "You're handing them our heads!"

Albert slowly lowered his gun and began to sob. "You're right, Ellsworth. It's over."

Then, before he could be stopped, Albert brought his gun to his temple and fired.

CHAPTER TWENTY-NINE

Samantha had the story, but she wasn't celebratory. Watching a man take his own life shook a person up. Poor Albert Oakes—such a tormented man.

However, the piece had to be written, and as promised, she'd offered to share the byline with Johnny, but he refused.

"You did most of the legwork on this one, doll," he'd said. "You deserve it."

Mr. August had given her a week off with pay, a sign that he appreciated her dedication. Normally, she wouldn't have accepted, but she had Talia to think of. Samantha was now enjoying special time with her daughter, wandering the Public Garden and enjoying the park's peaceful, early-summer beauty.

She'd invited Mrs. Berrymaple to join them. The poor lady had suffered several shocks, having been suspected of a serious crime and losing a friend to murder.

"Lovely day it is," Mrs. Berrymaple said. "It's nice the heat wave has ended."

Samantha agreed. She offered Talia the bag of dried bread bits she'd brought along to feed to the ducks, smiling when the ducks waddled close.

"Maybe you can explain some things to me," Mrs. Berrymaple said as they watched Talia toss bread-crumbs. "What happened to Mr. Benjamin Oakes? Tell me the whole story."

Samantha glanced at the woman and sympathized with her need to make peace with what had happened to her husband and with the man she'd found at fault.

"All right. Six years ago, Benjamin Oakes put his name and finances behind preserving Boston city's historical buildings and landmarks."

"Yes, that much I know."

"Of course," Samantha said, acknowledging Mrs. Berrymaple's work at the Society. "Well, according to Ellsworth, their butler, it was a time of unity between the brothers. Ellsworth, having been with the family from before the sons were born, had become a surrogate father figure despite retaining his role of service to them. He'd confessed to encouraging their new shared passion, which he expressed regret for now."

Mrs. Berrymaple straightened her hat. "How was he to know this path would eventually lead to their destruction?"

"Exactly. It was Benjamin who first came across the old handwritten letter penned by Mrs. Mary Oakes—"

"The one Mr. Turner told me about. Its contents pointed to a possible disruption in the Oakes family line."

"Yes," Samantha said. "Ellsworth claimed that Albert had been appalled by the concept and refused to discuss it. He'd demanded that Benjamin destroy the letter and leave his position with the Historical Society."

"Ah, and Ben refused."

"He became obsessed with finding the truth, no matter the consequences, even to the point of bullying the groundskeeper, Mr. Cole Sr. Ellsworth claimed he tried to mediate but found it impossible to remain neutral and sided firmly with Albert Oakes. To his mind, the truth was ruinous and must never be revealed."

"And yet . . ."

"Benjamin insisted they could keep the truth to themselves, but he, on a personal level, needed to know if he was the offspring of General Oakes or not."

"I can't say I blame him," Mrs. Berrymaple said with a note of reluctance. "If I were in his shoes, I'd want to know. Even if the truth was terrible, it's still the truth."

Samantha wasn't sure she agreed. Some skeletons were best left in the closet—unless, of course, a murder needed solving.

"Albert didn't agree with his brother," she said, "and they argued intensely for months until Ellsworth noticed that Ben never showed up for any meals, worked in his office, or performed any of his usual routines.

"Ellsworth questioned Albert, who mumbled something about Ben leaving for England. Albert wasn't a skilled liar, and Ellsworth finally got him to confess. According to Albert, the brothers had gotten into a physical altercation, which ended with Albert grasping for a weapon from the top of a desk, which sadly turned out to be a letter opener. Benjamin died from the attack. Albert panicked and dragged his brother's body down into one of the estate's many cellars."

Mrs. Berrymaple's gloved hand moved to her lips. "Oh, dear."

"Ellsworth confessed that he and Albert agreed that nothing would be gained by involving the authorities, that they would go ahead with the story that Ben had decided to move to England. The body would be left in the cellar and forgotten.

"Except that Albert's conscience wouldn't let him rest. He developed insomnia and carried tremendous guilt. He had disagreed with his brother, but he hadn't hated him. He loved Ben and felt his brother deserved better than to be forgotten and left in a dark, dank cellar."

Samantha waved her arm toward her daughter. "Talia, come closer!"

She waited until Talia returned, then finished the tale. "Ellsworth couldn't imagine what had gotten into Albert, only that, somehow, putting his brother's bones with those of Mary Oakes was a way of making amends for what he'd done. 'It was then,' Ellsworth was reported to have said, 'I knew he'd lost his mind.'"

Samantha felt it was time to change the subject, especially since Talia was now in earshot. "Are you going to continue with your work at the Historical Society, Mrs. Berrymaple?"

"I don't know. Maybe in the future. I've had enough excitement for a while. Besides, I like the work I do for you and Dr. Higgins. Oh—" Mrs. Berrymaple stared across the park. "Isn't that one of your gentlemen friends?"

Samantha looked in the direction Mrs. Berrymaple was gazing, her eyes landing on Johnny. Her heart warmed. "What is he doing here?"

"Looking for you, I think," Mrs. Berrymaple said. "He's coming this way."

"Well, hello, Miss Hawke," Johnny said with a smile. He tipped his hat. "Good afternoon, Mrs. Berrymaple." He caught Talia's eye and bent down to her level. "Good day, Miss Rosenbaum. I don't think we've been properly introduced. I'm Mr. Milwaukee. I work with your mother at the paper." He held out his hand, and Talia tentatively shook it. Something about the gentle interaction made Samantha feel joyous.

"I know," Talia said. "Mom has talked about you."

Johnny smiled, that adorable, crooked smile. "Only good things, I hope."

"Talia—" Mrs. Berrymaple reached out an arm

and took Talia's hand. "Let's you and I go watch the swans. Say goodbye to Mr. Milwaukee."

"Goodbye, Mr. Milwaukee."

"See ya around, Miss Rosenbaum," Johnny returned.

Talia giggled and skipped away with Mrs. Berrymaple.

Samantha appreciated Mrs. Berrymaple's discretion but thought it was probably unnecessary.

"Taking a day off, Johnny?" Samantha said. "Serendipitous that we should meet like this in such a large public place."

Johnny's grin faltered. "I'll be honest with you, Samantha. This isn't serendipitous. I called your place and Dr. Higgins told me you'd be here."

Samantha noted two things: first, Johnny had called her by her full first name, not Sam, not doll, not Miss Hawke. Second, her own chest had tightened. Had he come to deliver bad news?

"What is it, Johnny? Is something wrong?"

"It depends on your answer to this question. Will you go out with me? I like you, Samantha, a lot. I want to date you. Seriously."

Samantha felt blood drain from her face. This was exactly the conversation she'd dreamed of having with Johnny. Nothing would make her happier than strolling through this park, arm in arm, officially dating Johnny Milwaukee.

A smile tugged on her lips, but then she remembered, and it fell.

"What is it?" Johnny said. "Don't tell me you don't feel the same way, because I don't believe it."

"It's not that, Johnny," Samantha said, "but I have to tell you something first."

"Okay."

Samantha swallowed, her gaze leaving Johnny's face. She couldn't bear to look him in the eye when she told him the truth of what she'd done.

"I know about you and your wife, and your baby daughter. I searched your background through the records kept at the city hall. I know I shouldn't have done it. I had no right. It's just, I like you, but I have to be careful, for Talia's sake. Seth was a snake, and I couldn't risk letting myself fall for another man like him. And I know you're not like that—"

She felt Johnny's warm palms on her shoulders. "Samantha. It's okay."

Samantha dared to look at him. "What?"

"I understand." He grinned softly. "I'd expect nothing less from such an intrepid reporter as yourself. Besides, I was going to tell you as soon as I had a chance. If I'm going to date a woman properly, then she has a right to know."

"Oh."

"And, so you understand, I've never shared that part of my life with anyone before."

"Oh."

"Samantha. You are the most incredible, intelligent, wonderful woman I have ever met. I can't imagine my life without you."

"And Talia?"

"She's an extension of you. I miss my own daughter so much, every day, but being a part of your daughter's life would be a gift."

"Oh, Johnny." Samantha stretched onto her tiptoes. Johnny removed his hat slowly and leaned in. The kiss that followed would be one Samantha would remember for her whole life.

WHEN DETECTIVE BROCK asked Haley if she'd like to go out for dinner with him, she immediately thought the detective wanted to discuss the case. A way of wrapping things up emotionally, as, try as one might, it was impossible not to be affected emotionally in this line of work. People's lives were irreparably changed, and many ended up on death row.

Like Walter Ellsworth. He had given a full confession that answered most of Haley's questions. She had read the transcript. As it happened, in his search and discovery efforts regarding historical items and artifacts, William Turner had happened upon a second letter written by Mary Oakes. He'd made a mistake in contacting Albert Oakes, which was how Ellsworth came to know about it.

When Ellsworth learned that Turner was continuing the research into Mary Oakes and a probable child born out of wedlock, he decided to stop the man from talking. He said, "There's only one way to accomplish that effectively." With the promise of news of "historical significance," Ellsworth lured Mr. Turner to the cemetery and shot him there. When asked why he hadn't done the deed at the Oakes estate, the butler had shrugged. "I didn't want another body to take care of at the house."

It was just a silly coincidence that Mr. Cole Jr. had taken Mrs. Berrymaple's old trunk to the jumble sale at King's Chapel and that it happened to be conveniently sitting there in a pile with other jumble donations. Ellsworth used the trunk to transport Turner's body by car to the meatpacking plant to deposit it in the furnace—since he had Albert's key—but he hadn't heard that the new manager, "blasted Cromwell," had put in new security. When the lights flashed, Ellsworth panicked and ran, leaving the body in the trunk behind.

Ellsworth did solve the mystery of Ben Oakes' missing fingertip. "Lost it when he was a lad of ten. An unfortunate encounter with a hatchet while building a tree fort."

To Haley's surprise, Detective Brock told her he would pick her up at her apartment. She was ready to assure him that she could meet him wherever he wanted to eat, but he'd already hung up before she could do so. To further her surprise, Detective Brock arrived with a cleanly shaven face, wearing a newly pressed suit, and carrying his *new* hat.

"Detective Brock?"

"Please, call me Nolan. I think our friendship has progressed so far, hasn't it?"

Haley couldn't recall another time in recent history when she'd been repeatedly shocked by the same person in such a short period.

"Very well, Nolan. Then you must call me Haley."

Nolan smiled. "Haley."

Haley grabbed her purse and gloves, her hat already pinned to her barely tamed curls. She held out the crook of her arm, and Nolan weaved his into it.

"Am I to assume we are going on a dinner date and not to talk about the case?" Haley asked.

"Correctly deduced, Haley." He grinned as he led her down the stairs to the street. "Now, I understand you like Italian."

Haley felt her wide smile grow even wider. "I do, Nolan. I do."

ABOUT THE AUTHOR

Lee Strauss is a USA TODAY bestselling author of The Ginger Gold Mysteries series, The Higgins & Hawke Mystery series, The Rosa Reed Mystery series (cozy historical mysteries), A Nursery Rhyme Mystery series (mystery suspense), The Light & Love series (sweet romance), The Clockwise Collection (YA time travel romance), and young adult historical fiction with over a million books read. She has titles published in German and French, and a growing audio library.

When Lee's not writing or reading she likes to cycle, hike, and stare at the ocean. She loves to drink caffè lattes and red wines in exotic places, and eat dark chocolate anywhere.

For more info on books by Lee Strauss and her social media links, visit leestraussbooks.com. To make sure you don't miss the next new release, be sure to sign up for her readers' list!

Discuss the books, ask questions, share your opinions. Fun giveaways! Join the Lee Strauss Readers' Group on Facebook for more info.

Love the fashions of the 1920s? Follow me on Pinterest

Did you know you can follow your favourite authors on Bookbub? If you subscribe to Bookbub — (and if you don't, why don't you? - They'll send you daily emails alerting you to sales and new releases on just the kind of books you like to read!) — follow me to make sure you don't miss the next Ginger Gold Mystery!

Murder on Fleet Street

Murder at Brighton Beach

Murder in Hyde Park

Murder at the Royal Albert Hall

Murder in Belgravia

Murder on Mallowan Court

Murder at the Savoy

Murder at the Circus

Murder in France

Murder at Yuletide

Murder at Madame Tussauds

Murder at St. Paul's Cathedral

Murder at the Olympics

LADY GOLD INVESTIGATES (Ginger Gold companion short stories)

Volume 1

Volume 2

Volume 3

Volume 4

Volume 5

Volume 6

HIGGINS & HAWKE MYSTERY SERIES (cozy 1930s

historical)

The 1930s meets Rizzoli & Isles in this friendship depression era cozy mystery series.

Death at the Tavern

Death on the Tower

Death on Hanover

Death by Dancing

Death on Tremont Row

Death at King's Chapel

THE ROSA REED MYSTERIES

(1950s cozy historical)

Murder at High Tide

Murder on the Boardwalk

Murder at the Bomb Shelter

Murder on Location

Murder and Rock 'n Roll

Murder at the Races

Murder at the Dude Ranch

Murder in London

Murder at the Fiesta

Murder at the Weddings

A NURSERY RHYME MYSTERY SERIES(mystery/sci fi)

Marlow finds himself teamed up with intelligent and savvy Sage Farrell, a girl so far out of his league he feels blinded in her presence - literally - damned glasses! Together they work to find the identity of @gingerbreadman. Can they stop the killer before he strikes again?

Gingerbread Man

Life Is but a Dream

Hickory Dickory Dock

Twinkle Little Star

LIGHT & LOVE (sweet romance)

Set in the dazzling charm of Europe, follow Katja, Gabriella, Eva, Anna and Belle as they find strength, hope and love.

Love Song

Your Love is Sweet

In Light of Us

Lying in Starlight

PLAYING WITH MATCHES (WW2 history/romance)

A sobering but hopeful journey about how one young German boy copes with the war and propaganda. Based on true events.

A Piece of Blue String (companion short story)

THE CLOCKWISE COLLECTION (YA time travel romance)

Casey Donovan has issues: hair, height and uncontrollable trips to the 19th century! And now this ~ she's accidentally taken Nate Mackenzie, the cutest boy in the school, back in time. Awkward.

Clockwise

Clockwiser

Like Clockwork

Counter Clockwise

Clockwork Crazy

Clocked (companion novella)

<u>Standalones</u>

Seaweed

Love, Tink